Bivan's House

Kyuka Lilymjok

ISBN 978-978-954-755-5

Published by:
Free Pen Publishers
10 Lachlan Close, Maitama, Abuja

Any people depicted in stock imagery provided by Thinkstock are models, and such images are being used for such purposes only.

This book is printed on acid-free paper.

The views expressed in this work are solely those of the author and do not necessarily reflect the views of the publisher. The publisher hereby disclaims any responsibility for them.

To my wife Maria and my children: Justice, Sunfair and Fairprincess

Sneaky rat, oh shifty rat
Sneaks of theft, holes of spoils
Scurries for cover, tricks of escape
Squeaks of joy, squeals of terror
Thy plagues shall wind up
Upon thy head, oh foxy rat.

Chapter One

A rat stuck its head from under a pile of garbage stacked behind Talgon's office, darting its eyes left and right, listening to hear if anyone was still around the office premises. It was evening and most people who had offices in the same premises with Talgon had closed and gone home. But Talgon was yet to close and go home. His secretary used to his working late had long closed and gone home. But unlike Talgon's secretary, rats with holes in the undeveloped patch of land behind the office did not seem to get used to his late working habit. They never seemed to have the patience to wait for him to leave before they would emerge from their holes to forage for any food ingredient that might be lying around.

Hearing no noise, the rat that emerged from under the pile of garbage ran towards the building opposite Talgon's office which was used as a restaurant. Talgon sitting in his office with the door open saw the rat running towards the restaurant and he, more by reflex than any conscious decision, flung a pen he was holding at the rat. The rat hearing the sound the pen made when it hit the ground behind it made a hasty retreat back to the empty patch of land behind the office to wait for a more auspicious moment when, unseen by anyone, it would be able to make its way to the restaurant to scavenge for any chow that might be lying about.

Talgon had a strong distaste for rats. Of all rodents, he had more hatred and revulsion for rats. Every day when he worked late, he was bound to see a rat darting across his office towards the restaurant opposite his office. The rats always came out about this time when everyone except him had closed from work and gone home. Once he had tried evacuating the heap of garbage behind his office where he believed all the rats were hiding, but found many rat holes in the empty patch of land outside the pile of garbage. Expelling the rats under the heap of garbage therefore would not end the menace of rats around the office. Besides, the heap was such a messy sludge and he had such great aversion for rats that he would not want to encounter them while trying to eject them from the pile of garbage. His horror of turning up a rat and the nausea provoked by the messy garbage forced him to abandon the quest of dismantling the pile of garbage.

However, he was resolved now that somehow tomorrow, his cleaner and other menial workers in the neighboring offices must expel the rats behind the building that served as offices to different firms plying different trades and services. But even as he resolved, he saw little cheer in expelling the rats while the patch of land remained a dumping ground for refuse. If the rats currently there were flushed out or even killed, other rats would take their place as long as the land remained what it was. The waste collection board responsible for clearing the rubbish, like any government agency, would only remove the refuse when it had been bribed. That meant being bribed daily because the pile of junk sprouted up every day.

Four offices away from Talgon's office was a Day Care which was generating most of the garbage in the undeveloped patch of land with diapers popularly called *pampers*. The proprietor of the Day Care simply threw used *pampers* through the back window of her Day Care and thought nothing of it. Cobs of corn, waste papers, cartons and polythene bags that had migrated from far and near places had all found accommodation in the empty patch of land where they were all mixed up with the discarded *pampers* in a slimy sludge attracting rats and cockroaches.

During office hours, Talgon was tormented by the crying of babies from the Day Care. His only consolation was that most of the day when the babies would be crying, he was always out of the office seeking contracts. After office hours when the Day Care had closed, when he should have some quiet to think, rats attracted to the empty patch of land by discarded *pampers* thrown on the land behind the Day Care, excited into activity by the silence created by the closure of the Day Care, tormented him. It was like after parents withdrew their babies from the Day Care at the close of business, the rats were left behind to torment him.

The population of every living thing in nature is reducing but of rats, he thought. More than any other place, rats seemed to be crowding us out of these offices. These offices were recently painted, but look at what rats had turned them into. Behold I am about to do a thing around this premises which the ear of anyone that hears it shall tingle. On that day I will fulfill against all the rats in this premises all that I have being thinking against them.

After sitting on his seat for a while, he stood up and opened the small refrigerator standing near the wall of his office and took a bottle of fanta to drink. The only opener in the office was attached to his secretary's bunch of keys and she had carried it home with her. He first tried opening the bottle with his teeth, but could not. He carried another bottle from the refrigerator, wedged the caps of the two bottles against each other and flicked up the bottle he wanted to open, but the bottle did not open. The trick of taking off bottle caps with teeth or other bottle caps is the exclusive art of drunks, he thought. They alone know the right edge and angle to flick open a bottle. He went to the door and tried opening it by the lock slip-hole. Here he was more successful. There was a faint smile on his face while drinking the fanta. He was reliving an exchange with a friend in Konnasa club. His friend a member of Konnasa club had taken him to the club where he met other club members drinking beer. Being a teetotaler, he had accepted only a bottle of fanta from his friend. He diluted the fanta given to him with water and was drinking it in its diluted form when one of the club members who seemed to have seen for the first time what he was drinking cried out in protest, `someone has broken one of the ground rules of this club!'

'Which rule has been broken?' asked Talgon's friend.

'Your friend is taking fanta instead of something whisking,' said the man who protested.

'To make matters worse, he is even diluting the Fanta he is taking with water,' said another man.

'He is so heavenly minded as to be earthly useless,' added a third man.

At this Talgon fired back that the fellow who said he was so heavenly minded as to be earthly useless was so earthly minded as to be heavenly useless.

Everyone laughed at Talgon's witty reply.

As he sat sipping the fanta, another rat from the patch of land behind his office not hearing any noise darted across the office towards the restaurant in front of the office. On seeing the rat, Talgon quickly put down the glass of fanta in his hand and seized a piece of wood lying in front of his office and gave the rat a chase. The door of the restaurant was closed, but there was a little space between the floor and the door. When the rat got to the door it tried slipping into the restaurant through the space between the door and the floor, but proved too big for the space.

It should not happen that a rat should pass through the eye of the needle, Talgon thought.

Finding it could not slip under the door, the rat spun round in panic to run back where it came from. Talgon with a mixture of fear and revulsion jumped from the rat's path and aimed the piece of wood in his hand at it. The wood hit the ground behind the rat and jumped over it. The rat ran into the empty patch of land and slipped into a hole.

Talgon picked the piece of wood and dropped it again on the ground, shrugging his shoulders. He went back to his office and began sipping his Fanta once more. While sipping the Fanta, his mind dwelt on a supply contract he had secured from the state ministry of health. He has been awarded a contract to supply bedsheets to the state hospital in Bangora. He has executed the contract, but was flinching from the many pecking eyes that would fall on the money when he was paid. Virtually all the personnel of the ministry had demanded gratification from him. The commissioner called the ceremonial pot in Bivan's house – the nickname for Coastal Diamond the diamond-rich West African state, being the one that awarded the contract wanted twenty percent of the contract worth. The permanent secretary who helped to process the contract wanted five percent. The personal assistant to the ceremonial pot and even the messenger in the office of the ceremonial pot though did not insist on percentages wanted cuts for themselves because they said neither the ceremonial pot nor the permanent secretary would give them anything and they deserved something having played some role in facilitating the process of the contract to the point of award. According to the messenger, on Talgon's first visit to the ministry to bid for the contract, he was the one that opened the door to the office of the ceremonial pot and that had earned him a cut. The personal assistant claimed he was the one that kept reminding the ceremonial pot of his appointments with Talgon during the processes leading to the award of the contract and this has earned him his cut. Before, the ceremonial pot wouldn't have made his demand directly to him. He would have made it through the permanent secretary who was more involved in processing the contract and receive it through him. But things had changed in Bivan's house. It seemed no one trusted anyone any more in Bivan's house. It seemed the fear and honor that would have made the permanent secretary pass to the ceremonial pot his cut were both gone.

It was in *Wombe's Agony Column* the expression *Bivan's house* was first used as an epithet referring to the diamond-rich West African state of Coastal Diamond. Like a tie on a garbage bag, once the expression was used, it stuck. Now very few people could still remember this nation was once called Coastal Diamond.

Bivan was a great ancient warrior of the Kunsu tribe – the majority tribe of Costal Diamond. He was famous for his heroism and patriotic zeal to extend the frontiers of Coastal Diamond and have it as the greatest empire in Africa. He was killed in one of the numerous expansionist wars he fought; but not until he had established Coastal Diamond as a prosperous and secured empire.

Talgon has always found in the sobriquet *Bivan's house* a weeping irony for Coastal Diamond. For him it was a house for sale, a house for hire, a house for rent and a house for mortgage. He had a song for it:

> Bivan's house is for sale
> But it is being bought with dogshit
> Bivan's house is for rent
> But only lepers are seeking to rent it
> Bivan's house is for hire
> But only prostitutes are hiring it.
> Bivan's house
> The shit mountain of Africa.

According to legend, the origin of politics in Bivan's house was different from its origin elsewhere. In Bivan's house, politics originated from a society of headhunters.

The leader of the society of headhunters was called the primehead and so he who was called president or prime minister in other countries came to be called primehead in Bivan's house and what was called national assembly or parliament in other countries was called the house of archery in Bivan's house. A governor was the big feast, ministers were ceremonial feasts, ambassadors were close banquets, commissioners were ceremonial pots, local government chairmen were common calabashes and councillors were hunting bags. Like butchers said to have started surgery, legend had it that headhunters started politics in Bivan's house. According to legend, from its headhunting ancestry, politics in Bivan's house was to later evolve into a game played by people of the street whose battle cry was – *Loot all the food in the house into your hole whenever there is an opportunity to do so!*

To return to the contract Talgon was awarded, when the ceremonial pot was handing the contract allocation papers to him, he kept reminding him how lucky he was to have secured the contract as an outsider. Before, ministries rarely made tenders for bids to outsiders. The ceremonial pot awarding the contract tendered to himself, made the bid and awarded the contract to himself. But recently Abucham the big feast of Galiyo state had come out with a contract award procedure he called *Due Process* by which contracts were to be tendered to members of the public who made bids for them and whoever could show he had a better quotation, track record of performance and present ability to do a qualitative job than others won the contract. These were the official requirements Abucham the big feast insisted must be sold to the public. But behind these official requirements was the all-important requirement of the contractor's track record of giving the agreed kickback percentages to the contract awarders.

Talgon no doubt had given a good quotation and demonstrated competence. But so many other bidders had also met these requirements. But Talgon more than other bidders had a track record of quality job delivery. But the other bidders had a better track record of giving to the contract awarder his *due*. After giving process its *due*, the contract awarder expected his own *due* from the contractor and this was where Talgon was lacking, and this lacking was sufficient to deny him the contract, but for a word his uncle who was a ceremonial feast put in for him. He believed in doing a qualitative job and that by itself left him with only a marginal profit which if he were to give the contract awarder a *steak* – the popular name for a bribe in Bivan's house, the marginal profit that should be his own due from the contract would be wiped out.

The ceremonial pot had after the contract was awarded to him, called him to his office, in his words, to congratulate him for winning the contract.

'Thank you, sir,' he had said. 'I assure you, you will get value for money.'

'Yes, yes...yes,' muttered the ceremonial pot, his mind rolling what Talgon had said like a dice on a ludo plate. 'From a qualitative job the contractor also has his value,' continued the ceremonial pot, his eyes running over Talgon in a manner that tended to embarrass him. 'His quality job will fetch him more contracts.'

'That's true,' he said almost certain where the ceremonial pot was heading.

`If that's true as you said, the contractor who performed his contract well ends up with two *dues*: The *due* of a good job that fetches him other jobs and the *due* of a profit. The contract awarder is left with no *due* at all.'

'He enjoys the good name of insisting that contracts he awarded are duly executed.'

'Name?' murmured the ceremonial pot with a sarcastic expression on his face. 'What is the worth of a good name without money in Bivan's house?'

Chapter Two

'What is the worth of a good name in Bivan's house?' Talgon asked himself after leaving the ceremonial pot. 'What is the worth of honesty in this country?' While still in school, he did not write a particular paper during examination because he was sick. But the teacher mistakenly posted a result for him for the paper. He went to tell him that the result was not his because he did not write the exam. When members of his class heard what he had done, they not only jeered and booed him, but henceforth began to treat him like a leper. Very few students wanted to be seen with him. It was like honesty was a taboo and an abomination.

After school, he went into the army attracted by the discipline and incorruptibility he thought was in that institution. But he was soon disappointed into leaving the army when he saw junior military officers promoted over their seniors because they were protégés of high-ranking officers. Retired from the military, he got a job as a security officer in Gamubi University.

It was a security rule of the university that when students were returning to school with their luggage after vacation, they should show to the security men at the gate any electric appliance such as a refrigerator or television they were returning to school with. They were also required to show the purchase receipt of the appliance. The security men were required to register the appliance and endorse the receipt. If the receipt got lost, the student was supposed to report the loss to the security office so that he would be issued a pass for the appliance. A student was only allowed out of the university with any electric appliance if he showed an endorsed receipt or a pass for it.

As a security man, this rule was an inflexible one with Talgon and he applied it relentlessly. On one vacation of the university, a student going on vacation like other students drove a jeep to the gate with his friend sitting beside him and a television set on the backseat. He was stopped at the gate by Talgon. On finding the television set on the backseat, Talgon asked the student to show him the endorsed receipt for the television. The student had no receipt, but appeared unfazed. Part of the reason he had not put the television set in the booth of the car was that he knew that was the only place the robotic instincts of the security men at the gate would lead them to check. The backseat and any other place in the car were hardly checked by the security men. Even when they saw something on the backseat, they tended to ignore it and instead asked that the booth be opened as if that was the sworn abode of stolen items. Counting on this attitude of the security men of the university, he had placed the television set on the backseat confident he would drive through the gate with it without a query by the security men at the gate.

Now it seemed his forecast was wrong.

'I had an endorsed receipt, but lost it,' he said to Talgon.

'Where is your pass for it?'

'I have no pass.'

'Why?'

'Because your office has not issued a pass to me though I reported the loss of the receipt,' the student lied.

'To whom did you report the loss of the receipt in our office?' demanded Talgon.

The student did not say anything. By Talgon's attitude, it was fast becoming clear to him he had come up against a formidable circumstance. With his left hand, he brought out some money from his pocket and gave Talgon. Talgon collected the money and the student was beginning to smile to himself when he threw the money at him and demanded for his receipt once more. Shocked and bewildered, the student turned round to see if there was another security man he could appeal to, but there was no other security man at the gate. The other two security men at the gate had both gone to eat at a nearby makeshift restaurant.

'Take this money and let me go,' the student said, giving with the right hand this time the money he had gathered from the ground.

Talgon shook his head. 'Your receipt instead,' he said in a grating voice.

The student dipped his hand into his pocket

and brought out some new badun notes which he added to the ones Talgon had earlier rejected, put the money in an envelope and gave Talgon. But Talgon again rejected the money. It was now clear to the student that even if he were to give the jeep to Talgon as bribe, the security man would reject it and insist on the receipt. But his friend sitting beside him did not seem to think so. 'His money is his receipt; please take it,' he said, smiling slyly at Talgon.

'Shut up,' the student driving snarled at his friend, angered by his lack of recognition of their grave situation. He was seen in the school as the son of a rich man. But he was in fact an armed robber and the television set was one of the electronic gadgets he and his gang carted away in their last robbery operation. The present little incident could spark off a dangerous investigation.

But his friend did not shut up. Instead, he said, 'you look like you haven't eaten today. Take the money and buy yourself food and carry something to your wife and children so that you would be received well today when you get back home.'

Talgon was standing on the driver's side of the jeep. When he heard the student's yapping, he walked swiftly to the offside of the jeep, opened the car door and jerked the student out, holding him by the collar of his shirt. 'Can you repeat what you just said?' he breathed violence into the face of the student. He was a huge man who could tear the two students apart if it came to that.

The student now finding breathing difficult could not say anything.

'Whatever your master may be giving you, remember not to bark at everyone because if you do, you will be sorry when you bark at people like me,' Talgon said, pushing away the derisive student. Turning to the student driving, he again demanded for the receipt. At this point the two security men who went to eat joined him at the gate. There was now a long queue of vehicles at the gate and many people were beginning to honk their car horns in the exasperation of a hold-up. Talgon ordered the student to pull off the road to allow other vehicles pass. While the two security men who had just returned to their duty post were attending to the long queue of vehicles, Talgon was still demanding for the receipt of the television set. Though the other two security men heard his query, they did not concern themselves with it even after they had finished passing the long queue of vehicles through the gate.

The student knowing Talgon was not going to let him off without a receipt or pass approached the other two security men who turned out to be Talgon's seniors. After a little talk with these two security men, he offered them the money he had earlier offered Talgon. The most senior security officer at the gate snapped up the envelope containing the money the way a cat would snap up a rat. The envelope disappeared into his hip pocket. He stood up where he was sitting, pulling down his jacket to cover the bulge in his pocket made by the money.

'Yes, what is that man saying?' he asked as if he did not know what the problem was.

'He is saying I have neither receipt nor pass for my television and I told him I lost my receipt and had reported its loss to your office, but I am yet to be issued a pass,' the student said, fast regaining his confidence.

'Talgon, what he is saying is true,' the most senior security man said. 'I can even remember now that I was at the gate when this young man drove through this gate with the television. In fact, I personally endorsed his receipt.'

'If it is true he had a receipt for the television that was endorsed, but lost it and he had reported the loss to our office, to who did he report the loss and why has he not been issued a pass?' asked Talgon, a cloud of shock hanging over his face like the hood of a monk.

'Are you saying I am lying?' asked the most senior security man, looking mean.

'I am not saying you are lying. I am only concerned with the rules.'

The senior security officer nearly said he was the rules when he remembered he was not the chief security officer of the university. Irritated by this fact, he said, 'which rules? We make the rules and are therefore not their servants. Allow the young man to go,' he ordered.

'Well, if you say so.'

'I say so,' the senior security man said, looking evilly at Talgon. 'Even if this young man has never shown us any receipt for this television, that he owns this jeep should tell you he can buy a television.'

The student drove through the gate his eyes mocking Talgon.

Because Talgon saw the student giving his colleagues the money he had earlier rejected, after the student had driven away, they called him into the small cabin at the gate to share the money.

'You can share it between yourselves,' Talgon said. 'If I had wanted it, I would have collected it and pass him long before you returned.'

'You mean he offered this money to you before we came?'

'Yes, he did and I rejected it.'

'Something must be wrong with you,' said the most senior security man, contempt leaning out of his eyes to glare at Talgon.

After serving as a security man in the university for thirteen years, Talgon's reputation as a disciplined and honest man was established. Eventually he was made the chief security officer of the university. As chief security officer, he was appointed a member of a disciplinary panel set up by the university to hear and recommend disciplinary measures against security men accused of stealing some computers and stationery of the university. One of the accused security men came to his house one night with money begging him as a member of the panel to assist him in any way he could. He accepted the money without saying anything and the security man went home happy that he had compromised one of the panel members. If he could corrupt Talgon seen as the most incorruptible man on the panel, he was sure he could corrupt the other members. The following day when the security man who had given money to Talgon was called before the panel to defend himself of the accusation against him, Talgon did not allow him to say much before he said, 'the case of this man is a relatively simpler one. He has already confessed the crime he is accused of by giving me part of the money worth of what he is accused of stealing. Here is the money he brought to my house the previous night,' he said, handing over to the chairman of the panel the money the security man sought to bribe him with. After three years as the chief security officer of the university, his subordinates who bore the brunt of his demand for honesty were resentful of his leadership and plotted his downfall.

The Vice Chancellor of Gamubi University was a man of nature. People suspected he loved trees and animals than human beings. He was said to have once remarked that it always pained him when a human being is said to act like an animal. Asked why, he said it is an insult on the animal. Under his leadership, Gamubi University was turned into a huge garden of lawns and well-trimmed flowers. Once there was a delay in the payment of salaries of the university's laborers; the laborers threatened to devastate the flowers to hit back at the Vice Chancellor who they accused of using their salaries to irrigate flowers. In fact, some of the more incensed laborers did cut off some of the flowers. The Vice Chancellor on seeing the hacked flowers was livid with rage. Some laborers said he wept before the flowers like a child that was being weaned by his mother. The Vice Chancellor set up an investigation committee to fish out the culprits of the carnage on the flowers. When they were found, he summarily dismissed them from the service of the university. Those who knew Talgon knew that like the Vice Chancellor, he too loved trees and flowers. Perhaps Talgon even loved flowers than the Vice Chancellor, but because the Vice Chancellor was in a position to make his love for flowers keenly felt by members of the university community, it was his obsession that was more felt.

The security men who plotted to set Talgon up knew of the Vice Chancellor's and Talgon's love for trees. In their eyes, both Talgon and the Vice Chancellor were after the same mistress and they were going to use this mistress to pitch the two against each other.

'It is the thing that is sweet to a man that eventually kills him,' said one of the security men.

They all laughed at this comment.

The Vice Chancellor had an orchard in his house in which he had planted orange nurslings he brought from Israel. It was three of these orange nurslings that the security men pulled out from the orchard they were planted and put in the booth of Talgon's car. Talgon, driving home after close of work, without knowledge of what he was carrying in the booth of his car, was stopped at the gate of the university by the two security men at the gate. Usually, the booths of cars of members of the university community were not checked. But whenever there was a security lapse that led to theft or some other crime in the university, Talgon recognized no exception to the checking of cars. Then even the Registrar's car was checked. Members of the university community only resumed their privileges of being waved on at the gate without a check when apprehension over the security lapse abated. A week ago, the university's main internet cafe was broken into and most of its installations carted away. So everyone's car was checked at the gate.

Talgon opened the booth of his car and to his shock, three orange nurslings were found in the booth. The shock in his heart was branded on his face.

'*Ogar*, where did you get these nurslings?' asked one of the security men, enjoying Talgon's distress.

'Honestly, I don't know,' said Talgon. 'Someone must have smuggled them into my car.'

'But how could someone smuggle nurslings into the booth of your car without your knowledge?' queried one of the security men, his eyes mocking Talgon. Even before this incidence, Talgon knew this security man to be very rude. 'The booth of your car was not open. With your key you opened it before us. That means it is only someone with the key that opened the booth and put the nurslings there. You are the only one holding the key of your car and so must be the one that put the nurslings there.'

Shock and surprise made Talgon speechless for a while.

'Well, you know how much the Vice Chancellor loves trees,' said the other security man. 'Since these nurslings were apparently uprooted from the university, the matter must be reported to the Vice Chancellor for investigation. If we do not report the matter to him and he eventually learned of it, we will both lose our jobs.'

'The nurslings even look like those in the Vice Chancellor's orchard,' said the rude security man. 'Ah... this matter is turning out to be bigger than all of us. The Pope must certainly hear this one.'

This statement seemed to shake Talgon out of his paralysis. 'Well, you may report the matter to the Vice Chancellor if that is what you feel like,' said Talgon, shrugging his shoulders. 'All I know is that I didn't put these nurslings in the booth of my car.'

'The Vice Chancellor will be the judge of that,' said the rude security man. 'Ours is to report. His is to judge and punish.'

The security men reported the matter to the Vice Chancellor who literally ran amok when he went to his orchard and saw the three nurslings pulled out of the soil he planted them. Like at the gate, Talgon denied stealing the nurslings, but could not explain how they came to be in the booth of his car. Unlike previous Vice Chancellors who liked Talgon because of his honesty and incorruptible character, this Vice Chancellor was a very corrupt man that did not like Talgon. Talgon's honesty was like a mirror reflecting his dishonesty and he did not like that. He had thought of ways of easing Talgon out of the university without finding any. Though he suspected the nurslings to be planted in Talgon's car, the opportunity was too good to pass off. Talgon must go.

Talgon was sacked from the services of the university. Given the circumstances of losing his job, he did not look for another job. Instead, he decided to set up a small business of executing little contracts he could find. But he was finding the festering corruption in Bivan's house threatening to push him out of this means of earning a living.

The ceremonial pot who awarded him the

contract to supply bedsheets to the hospital seemed to wave honor away with the left hand and embrace corruption with the right. In a bid to get the twenty percent kickback he was demanding, he held him in his office until it was close to prayer time. It was a Friday and the ceremonial pot being a Moslem had to go for congregational prayers in a Friday mosque. There was no trick he had not pulled to get him committed to the twenty percent kickback, but Talgon would not make any commitment. He had a token appreciation to give after he had been paid, but would not tie himself to any percentage of kickback. Reeking with frustration, the ceremonial pot looked at his wristwatch and was surprised it was very close to prayer time. 'Ah...it's almost prayer time!' he exclaimed, standing up and running his two hands over his table apparently looking for something. 'How time flies!'

'Time is an eagle always on its wings,' said the permanent secretary of the ministry who had just walked in with a file in his armpit.

'It is a rat gnawing at one's life while he sleeps,' said Talgon.

Having found what he was looking for – a cell phone, the ceremonial pot hurried out of his office with his praying mat under his armpit followed by Talgon and other people. Why is everyone carrying his things in his armpit here? Talgon wondered. What are they carrying in their hands?

Outside his office, the ceremonial pot without charm and without atmosphere walked away from Talgon and other people without the siren that attends to charm and atmosphere. Looking a little servile and unkempt, his aide wiggled behind him like the tail of a dog.

At the gate of the ministry, Bamun a contractor who got the contract to supply medical equipment to a hospital sold his contract papers to the genuine contractor who did not know anybody in the ministry and who unlike Talgon had no one to recommend him to the ceremonial pot for the award of a contract. So he had to wait outside the gate of the ministry to buy the contract papers of anyone with patronage in the ministry to whom a contract had been awarded, but who had no means of executing it.

In his mind, Talgon was saying to himself, 'Perhaps I will be better off selling my own contract given the various kickbacks demanded from me.' The contract was so much infested with corruption that it seemed some of the corruption would seep into the bedsheets he was to supply and would eventually seep into the sick people that would lie on them, making them sicker. 'Corruption has more or less become a native of this country,' he murmured to himself. 'Sometimes I feel fighting the blight in this country is like throwing stones at the wind – you get nowhere with it. It is the same feeling I have when eating popcorn. When eating popcorn, I always have the haunting feeling of eating the air. As my teeth grind against each other, I seem to get hungrier.'

On his way home, Talgon was stopped by a crowd of policemen at a checkpoint. They were so many and spread out on the road as if he was a flood they were slamming the sluice gate against. Before, there were few policemen at the checkpoints and they did not have to deploy so much energy to stop a vehicle at their checkpoints. But because of the bribes they collected at the checkpoints, drivers, particularly commercial drivers rarely stopped when they flagged them down. Since motorists knew the checkpoints were now tollgates and not what they were supposed to be, they stopped at checkpoints only when compelled to. In their desperation to stop vehicles on the road, police often were driven to such maniacal actions that sometimes caused accidents on the road. Those less aggressive, but equally desperate, danced on the road or salute drivers to coax them into giving them some money. Knowing they were more likely to make money from commercial drivers, police at checkpoints were more desperate to stop commercial vehicles than private vehicles which for all they might not know might be carrying superior police officers or big politicians. Knowing police at checkpoints would demand money from them, commercial drivers, whenever they were embarking on a journey, had five badun notes which they dropped at police checkpoints as they sped past the checkpoints. One bus driver had even said the police were dogs and he always carried bones with him which he dropped at every checkpoint.

Talgon usually did not give money to police on the road whenever he was stopped. But sometimes he gave them money not as bribe, but out of pity of their condition. One of the policemen that stopped him now, he could recall was the policeman he gave five hundred baduns, two weeks ago.

'O.C, can't you recognize me again?' he said to the policeman leaning out of the window of his car.

'No, I can't; who are you?' asked the policeman, his bloodshot eyes giving him the appearance of an irredeemable drunk.

'I am the man that gave you five hundred baduns on this same checkpoint two weeks ago,' Talgon said.

'I still can't remember you,' said the policeman, his left hand scratching his sideburns. 'But can you repeat your performance to refresh my memory?'

Talgon smiled and began driving away.

The policeman looked at him, shook his head and began flagging down an oncoming lorry.

Near his house, Talgon stopped by stalls of fruits sellers to buy oranges. A man in a faded shirt and trousers was standing near the orange stall Talgon parked his car.

'Do you want to run me over with your rickety car?' the man in the faded clothes flared up, looking contemptuously at Talgon. 'Let me tell you, I have a car better than this your boneshaker.'

'Even if you have no car, I have no right to run you over with my car,' Talgon said in a voice that was neither friendly nor hostile.

The man could not say anything. It seemed this was not the reaction he expected from Talgon.

'You see, this is the problem with the poor of Bivan's house,' Talgon said, his voice sounding angry. 'They have been manipulated by the rich into hating themselves instead of those oppressing them. I am just a victim like you. Instead of being angry with the primehead of Bivan's house who has stolen the money that would have made your life better, you are angry with me who is just another victim like you.'

The man looked at Talgon vacantly for sometime before walking away without saying anything.

Chapter Three

Talgon sitting in his office sipping fanta on this day he chased a rat could recall all his recent and remote experiences with corruption and the pitiable attitudes of the poor in Bivan's house. As he sat reliving the past, a third rat that looked like the one he earlier chased emerged from the dirty patch of land behind his office and began to make its way to the restaurant the other two rats wanted to sneak into. Knowing he would not get anywhere chasing the rat, he merely stamped his feet on the ground where he was sitting and the rat spun round to head where it was coming from. Fed up with the rats' invasion of his quiet moments in the office, he quickly finished drinking the Fanta he had been sipping and stood up to leave. Picking his diary, he suddenly remembered he had a wedding to attend the following day.

A week ago, he had returned home to find an invitation card to a wedding ceremony lying on his center table. It was placed there by his wife who received it from the prospective bride. She was the daughter of a neighbor who Talgon knew had lived a wayward life. When he first heard she was about wedding, he wondered who the unfortunate man was. When he saw him, he was full of pity for him. He was a raw youth with no knowledge of the world beyond what he had read of it in books and what he heard of it from the experiences of others.

Not wary of any swindle he might be victim of, he was full of excitement and prodigious expectations where he should have been apprehensive and resentful. He was an excitable youth before whom was a prize others before him were not worthy enough to win. His excitement was matched only by the excitement of the bride who daily marveled at her rare fortune. From prospects of dying an old maid, she was ending up marrying a young handsome man of such approachable manners. This increased Talgon's pity for the innocent, unsuspecting young man.

The wedding was taking place in Bangora. It was a town with a population of about nine hundred thousand people. The town situated on a flat grassland was vulnerable to firestorms, floods and rainstorms. Like many Bivan's house towns of its size, it had more of rural features than urban. Donkeys carried tons of loads of various types of goods through streets and cows often competed for space with motorists and pedestrians on the streets. Commercial motorcyclists known as *bakonche* provided most of the town's transportation for the poor who constituted the majority in this poor northern town. Like most northern towns, Bangora was populated by Moslems and Christians with very few adherents of African religions.

Because the bride was the daughter of a neighbor, Talgon knew, he had to attend the wedding ceremony though he would rather have not. He never liked ceremonies because he rarely found the entertainment others found in them. Besides, his car which he would have driven to the ceremony had mechanical problems he was yet to fix. For the past two days, he had had to go to work by public transport. Boarding a bus in Bivan's house was a humiliating experience for everyone because the buses apart from being scraps swaying and rattling unpleasantly on the road were always stuffed to their brims and spilling over with human beings and goods of all kinds. Once in a while, a man carrying his sheep, goat or pig flagged down a bus and he and his beast were passed into the bus by the bus conductor to jostle for space with the human beings already sitting or standing in the bus. Because of this, most commuters preferred to be transported by motorcyclists. But the problem with the motorcyclists was that they were always under the charge of one narcotic drug or the other. Many people who patronized them often end up either in hospital or crushed to death by vehicles the motorcyclists by their recklessness had ran into. Talgon dreaded the motorcyclists like a plague and so he always boarded a bus with all its inconveniences whenever he could not drive his car. So, if he must attend the wedding ceremony as he had made up his mind to, he would have to board a bus.

Like every ceremony of its kind, this

ceremony which turned out to be ill-fated was to take place on Saturday. The specific time of the wedding reception was 2pm. But everyone invited knew the reception would not commence until 4pm or even later. The wedding day was a day of moderate temperature – one of those rare days it seems humans have a hand in priming the weather to such benignity that is so pleasing to the body and everyone's sense of wellbeing.

By the time Talgon and his friend Badaru with whom he attended the wedding reception reached the venue of the ceremony, it was full of people. There was such a huge crowd it seemed the whole town had turned out for the wedding. The bride and the groom were dancing and were being sprayed with money by the guests. The whole area the couple was dancing was littered with badun notes which two ladies were picking into plastic bowls. After dancing for sometime, the couple went back to their seats and the master of ceremonies replaced them at the center of the reception arena.

Like most weddings Talgon had attended, the bride was looking much happier than the groom. Her face gleamed with satisfaction and a smile that looked to Talgon like that of a victorious hunter who had just claimed his trophy hung on her lips like a lily spring. Though the groom did not look sad, he did not look happy either. In place of the look of fortune on the bride's face was something akin to an expression of discontent on his face. Was the cat let out of the bag too late for him to make a dignified retreat? Talgon wondered.

Not too long after the bride and groom returned to their seats, things began to happen. From the eastern part of the wedding reception venue with a high Moslem population, shouts of *Allahu Akbar!* could be heard. From the western part with a high Christian population, shouts of *the Lord's army shall triumph*! were heard. Upon hearing the various war cries, most of the guests to the wedding ceremony who countless times had been witnesses and victims of recurrent religious conflicts needed not be told what to do. They ran for dear lives. But some of the guests who were zealous devotees of their faith hoping to make heaven by killing an unbeliever attacked anyone within range who by his dressing did not look like an adherent of their faith. It was such guests that killed most of the guests at the wedding reception venue. As guests attacked guests, armed bandits from the east and the west swooped down on the wedding venue hacking people to death and setting houses ablaze. The period of this conflict being the dry harmattan season, the fire quickly spread and engulfed most of the town.

The cause of this religious crisis was an argument between Christian and Moslem students in Hamze University on who between Jesus Christ and Mohammed is the messenger of God and the savior of mankind. Unable to resolve the argument with their heads, the students decided to resolve it with their fists. The clash of the students in the campus spilled over into Hamze town and beyond. It was news of the crisis in Hamze that had filtered into the sleeping town of Bangora and war cries had gone out among adherents of the two faiths to defend their Gods.

Talgon was one of the people who tried to flee the venue of the wedding reception arena too late. An old man was knocked down by the stampeding crowd and was about to be trampled to death; but Talgon bent down to help him onto his feet. From behind he did not know what hit him. He fell down on his knees and tried to stand up only to be knocked down again. The last blow he felt before he passed out was a bat on his head.

Almost an hour later, Talgon came to. Aided by his hands, he gradually stood up. Now standing on his feet, he could feel a searing pain on his thigh and a throbbing pain on his neck and head. He looked at the thigh and saw a big wound there. He could not immediately say what caused the wound. The eyeglasses he was wearing had fallen off, but he did not even look around for them though they were medicated eyeglasses. He looked about him and was frightened by what he saw. He was the only one standing. Around him were charred bodies of men and women roasted or fried to death by believers in God out to defend him from human beings that wanted to destroy him.

It was clear that people were sprayed with petrol or kerosene before being set ablaze. Recently that was how victims of religious conflicts in Bivan's house were killed. Unbelievers as they were considered by those who killed them, it was like a victim was given on earth a baptism of what he was to meet in the hereafter.

As Talgon stood gaping at the gory scene around him, he heard the cry of a child behind him. He spun round and saw a little child of about three years struggling to stand up from under a heap of garbage. He limped towards the child to deliver him from the debris that wanted to bury him alive. He reached the child to find that one of his legs was entangled in a twisted cable and it was the thing that was holding him down as if to drown him in the pile of rubbish. Rather irritably he extricated the leg of the child from the cable and brought him out of the rubbish. It was then the child really began to cry. It was as if after being delivered of the rubbish, he was delivered to the liberty to cry. He shrieked and screamed despite Talgon's efforts to calm him. Holding the child by his right hand, he started moving about the charred bodies around him to see if anyone was still alive that he might help.

He found the bodies of the bride and groom not far from each other. He was able to identify them by their clothes which were only partially burned. The groom lay on his stomach, his left hand twisted under him while the right hand was stretched out towards the bride as if for a clasp. His left leg looked as if it was broken while the right looked as if it had snapped. His head lay sideways, his tongue which ants were already moving on hung out like the lame hand of a beggar on his begging bowl. His throat was at the angle the throat of an animal to be slaughtered is usually set – only in his case he was beyond slaughtering. All the handsomeness he observed in the groom that evening was gone leaving behind a hideousness that turned his stomach.

The bride not far from the groom appeared to have died with more dignity or at least more decently. She was stretched out on her back, her left hand flung wide while her right hand was by her side. Her wedding dress was not as badly burned as the suit of the groom. She seemed to have died more of shock than any injury inflicted by the religious fanatics. Though she had been dead for a while, the fear of death still hung over her face like a shadow film.

Talgon holding the little child by the hand probed further for a survivor he could help, but found none. Not far from the bride and groom, he saw a charred body that looked like that of his friend. A tear dropped from his eye. A wedding where love is sown, some people had come and sowed hatred, he thought feeling very sad. Where life is sown, believers in God had sown death. The solemnization of an institution God ordained as the cornerstone of society, God's apostles had desecrated.

Carrying the little child now in his arms, Talgon decided to go home. Although he knew he would hardly get a vehicle to board because of the religious riots, because of the child and the injury on his leg, he waited for a while by the roadside for a bus or even a motorcycle to take him home. But as he expected, none came. Whenever there was a crisis of this magnitude, vehicles kept off the road, sometimes for two days or even more. Seeing no vehicle would come even if he waited the whole night, he began limping home with the child in his arms. The child was no longer crying. For the moment, he seemed to have come out of the shock of the attack. Not long after Talgon carried him in his arms, the child fell asleep.

Chapter Four

Moments after Talgon left the wedding arena, his friend Badaru who was hit on his head, but who like Talgon was lucky not to have been killed stirred on the ground where he had been lying unconscious. In pains and on giddy legs, he gradually rose up like a phoenix from the ashes of the mayhem. He was petrified by what he saw. Dead bodies littered everywhere and everything around him was still. It was as if the very air in the arena was dead because it was not stirring in any sensible way. Moving from where he rose up into the mass of dead bodies, he saw the bodies of the bride and the groom who, like Talgon, he was able to identify by their dresses. What of the money the bride and groom were sprayed with when they were dancing? What of the gifts they received? he wondered on seeing the dead bodies of the couple. What had happened to these treasures? They were not likely to have been carted away by the guests at the wedding reception who survived the mayhem given the suddenness of the attack and the confusion it created. Running for dear life not many people would think of dear money. As for the fanatics who came from outside, they did not know that so much money was sprayed on the couple and so would not go looking for it. So there was a chance the money or at least some of it might still be found. He started walking towards where he saw the money being tied into bundles shortly before the invasion. On his way to where he hoped he would find the money, he came across Talgon's eyeglasses and immediately recognized them. Not far away from the glasses, there was a badly burned corpse which he thought must be that of Talgon. 'So, he is dead,' he murmured. 'He must have been trying to help someone else when he had his own. Thank God I survived it.' He picked the eyeglasses and moved on. He got to the place he thought the money was likely to be lying around if by any miracle it had not been looted by the fanatics. Human corpses, empty juice packets, cans, water bottles and sachets, torn cartons, smashed food flasks, crates, fast food containers, spilled food, broken wall clocks and other mutilated gift items were strewn all over the dusty area the bride and groom were sitting before the attack. In the fading light of dusk, Badaru could not see any money in this mass junk. When he did not see anything by looking, he started clawing through the rubbish around him. It was then he turned up a wrap of money; but it was a charred wrap. He was very sad and disappointed. He threw the charred wrap away so that its presence does not continue to torment him. He continued to scratch around hoping to turn up unburned money. Almost when he had lost all hope of finding any money that was not destroyed by fire, he found a big wrap of money covered by dust and pieces of burned cartons. This bundle of money was not burned in any way. He was jubilant. He quickly tucked the money into his pocket and continued the search. But he did not find any money again. A bit disappointed, he stood up from where he had been crouched searching for the money to leave and go home, if home was still there for him. His home might have been set ablaze by the fanatics. But as he was walking away from the wedding arena, he remembered the wedding rings on the fingers of the couple. They would surely be worth a fortune from what he saw of them. Quickly he walked to where the bodies of the bride and groom were and removed the rings from their fingers. Dark as it was, he could only see the rings dimly and so could not say whether the attack had taken away some of their value. As he turned to leave the wedding arena finally, he heard someone in severe pains crying, 'I am dying; who will help me?' Apparently, someone the fanatics did not kill was coming around and needed help. Badaru bit his lips, shook his head and walked hurriedly away from the place.

Since Talgon left the wedding reception arena with the child, he had so far met only two people and these two people were policemen on patrol. The two policemen – a corporal and a constable, had been sent out with many other policemen to keep the peace that now sat uneasily over the town. Except for occasional flares of light from random bonfires kindled by rioting fanatics who had been dispersed by the police, the whole town was in darkness. The power supply corporation of Bivan's house has since become a black hole into which billions of baduns had been sunk without any improvement in power supply. However, successive Director Generals of the corporation had become fabulously rich. The last Director General of the corporation who came from the same town with Talgon had recently been given a chieftaincy title of *Sikumu Dai* meaning warrior of his town. He was hailed as a savior by the poor who often had to stay for more than five days without power. Because of failure by the power supply corporation to supply power and the Water Board to supply water, for most towns and cities in Bivan's house, light at night was supplied by either the moon or stars or by noisy electricity generating machines. As it was with light, it was with water. Drinking water was supplied by the sky during rainy season and by wells and rivers during the dry season. Often, whenever the power supply corporation or the Water Board of the sky were not on duty, there was no light or water for most residents of Bivan's house. Two weeks ago, the only place water could be found in Bangora was the Water Board. He like other residents of Bangora had gone to fetch water from the Water Board. When he got to the Water Board, there was a very long queue of people who had also come to fetch water. Prepared to spend most of the day at the Water Board, he joined the queue. Not long after, a man looking well off came and tried jumping the queue by taking his big water jerry cans to the front of the queue. Most of the people on the queue afraid to challenge him because he was apparently richer than them, said nothing. It was only when Talgon challenged him that almost everyone on the queue joined in objecting to the man jumping the queue. In frustration the man had to go and take his proper place on the queue, but not without throwing a contemptuous stare at Talgon. After sometime, the man in front of Talgon said very soon he would sink his borehole and be free of this misery.

'If everyone sinks a borehole, there will be no water in your borehole,' Talgon said.

The man then was returning the greetings of a woman who had just come to the Water Board. Because he did not say anything to what Talgon said, it was not clear if he heard what was said or he did not. Talgon thinking he did not, said after sometime, 'you dig your borehole and let everyone die, is that it?'

'I am not the government,' the man said. 'I cannot possibly sink boreholes for everyone.'

'But you can protest so that the government ensures that the Water Board does the job it was set up to.'

'Protest is by the masses led by the elites,' said the man. 'There are masses, but there are no elites to lead them.

Look at yourself. You have legs, a trunk, arms and a neck. But none of these masses of your body is useful for anything without the leadership of your tiny commander-in-chief – your head. A mosquito may be feasting on your leg; unless your head moves your hand to swat it, the mosquito will continue feasting on you until you drop dead from malaria or anemia. The masses of any country are headless and tailless. For them to commit themselves to any worthwhile struggle, they must be led by a head. The elites are that head.'

What the man said sank into Talgon like an iron hook with many spikes. For a while he could not say anything. 'It is bad,' he said at last.

'It is indeed bad.'

'The head will always be the capital and the rest of the body the labor responding to the command of the capital.'

'In what you just said I can see fresh problems for Karl Marx. His idea of labor dictating terms will forever remain utopian. For how can the body ever revolt against the head? Even when the head goes mad, it has a way of controlling the body. Labor lame and tame heeds only the sting of the whip on its back. It may bay at the moon, but it will not bark at capital – the whip on its back.'

'Yet, elsewhere the body protests against the head whenever the head passes pain to the body.'

'The body in those places you talk of has once upon a time, by some capital, been made to understand that the head like a pot on a hearth, sits on it and that without it there would be no head. The body in those places knows it is the roots and stem of the tree and the head is its mere outgrowth. The body here does not enjoy this awareness.'

'Without protest the commonwealth is gone forever and all we may hope for are private fortunes we can make to generate our individual comforts.'

'That's our miserable condition. In this country, the government is dead or sick at least. All those things the government is supposed to provide for the people, people have to provide for themselves. For most people in Bivan's house, electricity has become a nuisance. Always it is not there and when you are getting used to its absence, it is flashed at you to remind you that you ought to have it. In most homes that can afford it, electricity at night is supplied by noisy generators that have turned the whole country into a madhouse.'

'We don't have light, we don't have water, we can barely feed ourselves, but we are fighting over God,' lamented Talgon.

'Perhaps we are fighting over God so that he can fight the government we cannot fight.'

'According to a friend, our condition will continue to deteriorate the longer we stay in darkness because of lack of electric light,' Talgon murmured, sheepishly. 'He said when you stand in the dark for too long, some of the darkness will enter your head and you can't see clearly even in the daytime. When you look at mud for too long, some of the mud will enter your head through your eyes so that what is crystal clear to others is as clear as mud to you. When you live in the forest for too long, some of the forest will enter your mind and you will start sharing the thoughts of the monkey. He said it is a mystical thing he cannot explain, but that it happens.'

'We are in for it.'

'Not even the donkey can dispute that fact with you.'

For a while Talgon lapsed into deep thought. When the man said he was not the government, in a sense he was right; but in a sense he was wrong. He was not the government in the sense that he had no obligation to provide water and electricity to anyone. But he was the government because he had to generate his own water and electricity. Because government has failed to generate commonwealths from which the people can draw, whoever he spoke to in Bivan's house was always possessed by a sickening quest of heaping up personal wealth to provide some comfort for himself. There was nothing sick about making money or acquiring wealth by application of industry. But what he found sickening about members of Bivan's house obsession with wealth was that they dreamed of making money not by their efforts, but by bleeding the country white. When the opportunity offered itself and a member of the house found himself in a position of stealing public money, he was hailed by those he was stealing their money as *making it*. It was so sickening to him.

'But, why can't the poor in this country link their misery to the stupendous wealth of the rich?' he wondered aloud.

'Because like the rich, the poor are corrupt,' said the man behind him.

'I can hardly dispute that with you,' Talgon said with a note of bitterness. 'You know the complaint of people from the diamond-rich Mapuka region is that they are marginalized in corruption. Recently, they have being saying that unlike people from other parts of the country they are not allowed to have their fair share of corruption. When Sokari a big feast from that region was prosecuted for embezzling his state money, his people cried out that he was being persecuted; they were being marginalized in corruption. We do not hate corruption. We envy the corrupt. When you envy a thing, you don't attack it; you try to be like it. When you hate a thing, you kill it.'

'You are beginning to see things the way they are,' said the man.

Now walking in the darkness that hung over the town like a smoke-puffing monster, Talgon was disturbed by the silence that oozed out of the town like a creeping menace. Usually after a clash like this, people who survived it kept off the streets not knowing who was out there that one might fall victim to. The two policemen he met on the road stopped him to perform their duty of keeping law and order. The corporal by his attitude gave law and order the face of an ill-tempered dog that was growling at him in a chilling way that could make the hair of a lily-livered man stand on end. Seeing he was an injured man carrying a child in distress, who by the frailty of his limbs and the burden of the child he carried held no danger for law and order, the two policemen nevertheless heckled him with questions.

'Where are you going?' the constable asked, turning his torchlight on him.

'To my house.'

'Why are you out of your house at this time on a night like this?'

'I went to a wedding ceremony at Durmi and was caught by the crisis there.'

'Why did you attend the wedding?'

'Because I was invited.'

'Why were you invited?'

Talgon did not say anything.

'Can you show us your invitation card to the wedding?'

'I left it at home,' said Talgon.

'Why did you leave it at home?'

'I didn't know I would be asked to produce it on the road.'

'Why did you not know you would be asked to produce it on the road?'

Again, Talgon did not say anything.

'I rather think you were not invited to the ceremony?'

'I was invited,' said Talgon.

'All those invited to wedding ceremonies have invitation cards; where is yours?'

'I was not only invited with a card, but by radio.'

'You see; this is what I have always lamented in this country. The culture of inviting the whole world to ceremonies through the radio makes our job of maintaining law and order in such ceremonies more difficult. It is what leads to great loss of lives if there is a crisis like this. For attending a wedding on a radio invitation, we can charge you for wandering.'

'But I am not wandering. I am going to my house with a sick child,' said Talgon in panic.

'Yes, the child. Why should you take a small child like this with you to a wedding ceremony?'

'He is not my child. I found him in the battue the wedding arena was reduced to.'

'He is not your child?' asked the corporal in a voice laced with suspicion.

'Yes, he is not my child.'

'You will have to follow us to the station. We suspect you are a ritualist who steals people's children for moneymaking rituals.'

'If I were, I would have told you the child is mine.'

The constable more accessible to reason

found this defense plausible. But it made no impression on the corporal who was almost convinced that Talgon was a ritualist. 'People use their own children for moneymaking rituals,' he said in a voice that carried his conviction.

'Well, I am not a ritualist to start with,' Talgon said in a grave voice.

'Who are you?' asked the constable.

'I am Talgon.'

'You are Talgon?' said the constable more as an expression of surprise than a question.

'I am Talgon.'

By a fortuitous coincidence, a security man in Gamubi University who was an uncle to the constable had told him about Talgon and how honest a man he was. 'Where do you work?' he asked Talgon.

'I am a contractor,' said Talgon.

The constable for a while did not say anything. He was wondering whether it was the same man his uncle told him about or not. But his uncle said Talgon was sacked by the university. It was possible that after he was sacked, he became a contractor. 'Have you always been a contractor all your life?' he asked Talgon.

'No,' said Talgon, wondering where all these questions were leading to.

'What were you doing before you became a contractor?'

'I was a security man in Gamubi University.'

'Wonderful!' cried the constable. 'So you are Talgon the only honest member of Bivan's house? You are such an honest man that when your name is mentioned in hell, even the devil will object. You have a big and clean name, move on.'

Talgon was surprised by the attitude of the constable towards him. The corporal was angered by it. So angered was he that he walked away from where the constable and Talgon were. Ordinarily he would have stopped the nonsense the constable was engaged in and squeezed Talgon. But Talgon did not look like a cash-cow he could squeeze something out of. It was foolishness squeezing the tail of a cow for milk.

Chapter Five

Talgon limped forward perplexed by the behavior of the constable. Carrying the sleeping child in his arms, with a thumping pain on his neck which was aching him less and a big wound on his thigh which was aching him more, he could not move as fast as he would have wished. Several times he had to stop to fight a faint feeling that kept making him stagger as if he would fall. It seemed he had lost a lot of blood from the wound on his thigh. His only relief was that the child was asleep. If he were awake and crying, things could have been really desperate. He hoped he would be home before the child woke up so that his wife, if she had not been killed by the fanatics, would find something for him to eat. Whose child was he? he did not know. Had the child's parents been killed by the fanatics? he did not know. Whatever happened, nothing must happen to the child. If he must die, let him live to get the child to where he can find help.

Because Talgon walked slowly, his friend Badaru soon caught up with him. Like Talgon, he had looked for a car or motorcycle to take him home but did not find any. Like Talgon, he decided to trek home. As he walked, his right hand never left the pocket the money he stole from the wedding reception venue was. Throughout his life he had never owned this kind of money. Now he was going to be somebody if he was able to manage the money well. The two policemen Talgon met on the road, he did not meet. By the time he got to the point Talgon met them, they had left that road and gone to another part of the town. So Talgon was the first person he saw on his way home. He was surprised seeing him. He had thought either everyone in the town was dead or was so badly injured or frightened by the religious mayhem to venture out of doors. Who then was the phantom looming before him? Who ... who could it be? What could it be? A spirit? A ghost? It was a ghostly night and it was very much likely that the figure ahead of him was a ghost. Who in his right senses would venture out of doors in such a night? His pace fell. He must not walk past the figure ahead of him. Two options presented themselves to him: He either continues walking at the pace he was which would keep him permanently behind the figure until they parted ways or leave this road and take another road. He favored walking behind the figure. Who knows who or what he might run into if he leaves this road and goes to look for another?

Talgon with the sleeping child in his arms limped on. Would he be able to make it home feeling the way he was? he kept wondering. If only he had his cell phone with him. He would have called his wife and told her his condition so that she would not be unduly worried. But he had forgotten the cell phone at home when he was going for the wedding. He never seemed to get use to the cell phone as to always remember to carry it with him wherever he was going. There was a religious uprising; there was no telephone vendor on the street he could call his wife's number by his phone. With a sinking feeling he suddenly realized he did not even know his wife's number by heart. So even if he could find a telephone, he had no number to use except his own which might not even be useful to him because he suspected the battery of his cell phone had ran down. The town as quiet as a graveyard had acquired the eeriness of a graveyard. It was either that everyone was dead, too sick or fearful to come out or even speak. He had never heard or seen this kind of disaster. The images of charred bodies he left behind kept riveting in his mind as much as he tried pushing them out. Human beings reduced to fingers-crushable charcoal by fire from the hands of fellow human beings, could anything be more harrowing? Who looking into a church or mosque would think these citadels of faith could kindle this kind of fire? How do we come to be caught between two lakes of fire – one above kindled by the devil to roast sinners and another below kindled by believers in God to roast unbelievers? Ah... this leg. If only there was someone near to help this child. Perhaps he should have held onto the policemen he met on the road, particularly the constable. His right leg with the wound now felt like lead and taking it along with him was proving torturous. Though it was night and not hot, he was sweating profusely. When the pain in his right leg became unbearable, he stopped walking and gently laid the child on the ground beside the road and tried to sit down to rest. As he tried sitting down, a stab of pain shot through his wounded leg making him cry out. Was it only the wound or had he sustained a dislocation or worse – a fracture? He was now really scared. If he could not get home before the child wakes up, both he and the child would be in a very pitiful condition. But the child has not moved for some time now. Even when he was laying him on the ground, he could not remember the child moving. Was the child dead? His heart skipped a beat and more sweat poured from his face. He leaned over and shook the child and he stirred then began to cry. Now he had woken up a storm when he had nowhere to enter.

Badaru did not realize Talgon had stopped walking until he cried out when he was trying to sit down to rest. Talgon's cry jolted him almost like an electric current. The quietness of the night and the anxieties welling in Badaru combined to give the cry a shrillness and eeriness that shook him into uttering a little cry of his own. His fears were confirmed. A ghost was ahead of him. The cry of the child after that of the figure dispelled all doubt. A ghost all at once can cry as a baby, a man, a woman and even as a cat. He would have to find another road to get back home. He had better leave while he could. He turned and walked back a little and took a dark alley he was not sure where it was leading him.

Talgon, with the child once more in his arms was mumbling a lullaby to lull the child to sleep again. But the child continued to cry. How he wished he had a *mondo* with him. With a *mondo*, he knew the child would go back to sleep or at least become quiet the moment he began playing it. Like his friend Badaru, he was also on the verge of a decision. He would not be able to reach home with the child feeling the way he was. How could he when he could hardly lift his right leg from the ground? He must seek and find help. He could sit where he was and cry loudly until help comes. But that would be unmanly and his unmanliness would return to haunt him after he had recovered from his current distress. For present relief, a man should not do what he would later be ashamed of when a current distress has abated. The time was not even for crying. Crying in a day of tribulation and agony like today would not have on anyone the effect it would on a normal day. What the people saw today, crying aloud would only bring succour to anyone hearing such a cry that there were still people who could cry instead of being a call for help – a Mayday. Holding the child under his right arm, he tried standing up. Another stab of pain shot through him. Biting his lips, he steeled himself against the searing pain and stood up with the child. He looked round him and saw a house with a hurricane lantern burning in the living room.

Should he go to the house with the lantern and seek help? he wondered. But he might be killed if the owner of the house considered him an unbeliever in his faith. But he could not make it home the way he was. And there was the child he was carrying. If he would not reach home and find succor soon, the child would suffer and perhaps perish with him. He must take a chance with the house. He began limping towards the house.

Chapter Six

As Talgon moved towards the house, the sky in front of him caught fire and burned for a while before it ran out of fuel. When it ran out of fuel, the fire burned out and like a thatched roof that had burned out, the ashes fell upon those under the sky where the fire burned. It was a very awesome and frightening thing while it lasted.

It was as if the maimed and sick in the town were waiting for the sky to catch fire for them to mobilize the remaining strength in them to cry out for help. As the fire in the sky was about burning out, many tortured minds and fractured hearts in united terror cried out in a prolonged roar of agony.

Some religious fanatics not content they had done enough to show the power of God on earth had regrouped in the outskirts of the town to torch up the skies by using long water pipes to which they had tied kerosene-soaked straws. They lighted the straws, raised the water pipes into the sky and waved about what they called *the flags of God*. If the flaring flames from *the flags of God* would not move infidels to have faith in God, then nothing would.

Talgon was awe-stricken by the tongues of fire that licked the sky like a wild bushfire. 'What is it? What is it?' he cried. 'Both the sky and the earth are speaking to men in tongues and floods of fire.' He felt listless and threatened. But he also felt a little hopeful. From the outcry that followed the burning sky, there were many survivors of the religious carnage. Together they would pull out of the catastrophe. If only he had his *mondo* with him. This was the type of moment to play a healing tune on a *mondo*. Before he goes to sleep, he must somehow find or improvise a *mondo* and calm the town to sleep. He was in pain no doubt. But he was only one person out of thousands. What was his pain compared to the many thousands whose types of pain he did not know? Many were dead. Badaru with whom he went to the wedding was dead. 'My poor friend,' he wept. How could they have gone to the wedding together only for him to return alone? 'Oh, this life! What is it worth if a man would not be of use to his fellow man?'

He was now feeling his life was spared for him to help others, not grieve over his own injuries. If only he could have a *mondo*. If only he could find something for this child to eat. He quickened his pace towards the house with the burning lantern.

When he got to the house, he called out on any soul in the house to come out and rescue a man and a child in distress. After a long while of standing in front of the house repeating his call for help, a woman came out holding the lantern that attracted him to the house. She placed the lantern on a table standing on the veranda of the house. It was a very bright lantern. It pushed back the darkness he was standing in and illuminated the frontage of the house.

Now he could see a man lying on the ground not far from the veranda of the house. The man had a head, but his face was gone. The riots went with it. A shudder went through him as he stood looking at the man without a face. By his left, there was a fresh hole it was difficult to tell what dug it.

'In what way may I help you?' the woman asked Talgon with frank hostility.

Talgon looked at the woman. She was standing where the light of the lantern fell directly on her face. Her eyes were twinkling like glow-worms – those little stars of the swamp in a dark night. Her eyelashes like roses in a valley gave her face power and charm that was gripping. Her nose rising from the valley of her eyes like a budding plant hung over her lips like a little cliff commanding the waters of a quietly flowing river. Her lips were supple in their rise and sensual in their poise. Cornrows on her head gave her the natural charm of a lawn in the wilderness and the holy presence of a visiting angel. Her eyes, nose and lips embraced each other in a feverish tangle of beauty that chimed like water at boiling point. Looking like a mermaid, she seemed to have dropped from the sky or as meet her mermaid appearance, she seemed to have come out of the sea after the mayhem had come and gone. The sweep of her facial beauty was such as to sweep any man off the sway of his morals. She moved a few steps from the lantern and stopped. There was such liquid grace and ease in her movement that had Talgon gaping at her, breathlessly.

'In what way may I help you?' she repeated her question in a stiff, brittle voice that was a sharp contrast to her grace and ease of movement.

'We are victims of the religious mayhem fleeing home from Durmi where we were attacked by religious fanatics. But we cannot reach home because the wound the fanatics inflicted on me is paining me severely and the child with me is equally distressed,' Talgon spoke rapidly, wary of the woman's stiff manners.

'As you can see, I have problems of my own,' the woman said in a brittle voice.

'I have seen him. It is so awful. But you can still help the child. I don't care about myself, but the child is very sick and I think hungry. Please, if you have any food, give him,' he beseeched the woman.

'Why should I help you? Nobody has ever helped me in my life. Look at my husband,' she pointed at the man lying on the ground. 'He has been lying there since his face was taken away by the religious inferno, but nobody, including me, has cared to help him. If I were the one so maimed, he also wouldn't have helped me. The world is so mean and I am learning fast the only lesson it has taught me.'

Talgon was shocked to hear the woman said she had not tried helping the man she said was her husband. What was the world coming to? he wondered fearfully. 'This child is sick and needs food,' he said, his mind turning to the child. 'I was taking him to my house to attend to him, but a big wound on my thigh prevented me. I saw light in this house and decided to come here to seek help of the inhabitants of the house. Please, help madam.'

The woman stood on the veranda saying nothing. Tired of standing, Talgon holding the child sat near the hole the lantern had illuminated. Sitting near the hole, he had the haunted feeling of sitting over it and the funny feeling that the hole was gaping into him. 'Did you say the man lying there is your husband?' he asked the woman, taking off his mind from the hole.

'Yes, he is my husband.'

What type of world are we living in? Talgon wondered again. A woman talking so coldly and callously about her husband who had been wasted by religious fanatics was something he found chilling. But whatever he thought of her manners, he had to admit she was beautiful in a rude and urgent manner. Perhaps some of the rudeness of her beauty has spilled into her manners, he thought. Her husband was now without a face he could compare with hers; but whatever was his face, he had a beauty as a wife.

'I understand how you feel,' he said. 'But we are talking about a child who is innocent of the meanness of the world.'

'If he is innocent, what of his father that will take the benefit of my help?'

'That's where you are mistaken; I am not the father of this child. I only rescued him from the religious mayhem that nearly claimed his life.'

'Whose child, is he?'

'I don't know.'

'And you are walking around looking for food for him? You may be charged by the police for ritual killing.'

'I can't watch him die of distress and hunger if I can help him. His parents perhaps were killed by this disaster.'

For a while the woman stood looking at him saying nothing. 'If what you are saying is true,' she said at last, 'you are like my father and I can tell you, you will only live a life of regret.'

'Perhaps you are right. But I will suffer more regret if I can't help this child.'

'No use,' the woman hissed. 'You can't be helped. My father was like that to his death. Life was scowling at him, but he was smiling at it. It was hissing at him, but he was kissing it. Pissing on him, he was missing life. He couldn't be helped and I can see you can't be helped either. But I will help the child.' Snapping on the light of her cell phone, she went back into the house.

Sitting in front of the house, Talgon's eyes kept straying to the man lying on the ground without a face. Looking at the man and the hole near him, he had the queer thought that what ate the ground ate the face of the man.

The woman came out with a small loaf of bread and water and gave the child who was now awake.

Though Talgon heard what the woman said earlier about not helping the man lying on the ground without a face, thinking perhaps he did not hear her right, he asked pointing at the man on the ground, 'what of him? You don't seem to be taking much care of him.'

'He wouldn't have helped me if I were in his position; why should I help him?'

Talgon's despair appeared on his face. What manner of woman is this? 'And you said he is your husband?' he asked.

'Yes, he is,' she said in a cold, flat voice. 'But I can't die for him. Even his mother would not die for him. Our hearts might be broken, but we all hold to our heads.'

'As your husband, you are supposed to be one. His suffering should be your suffering, his death your death.'

To Talgon's shock, the woman laughed. 'That's an insane piece of theology, isn't it? As you can see right now, his suffering is not my suffering and his death will not be my death. That proves the joke in your proposition.'

Talgon could only stare at her. Even the child who did not understand what she said was staring at her with what looked like shock.

'Life is a walking lie!' Talgon exclaimed at last.

'And a smiling fraud you should have added,' said the woman.

'It is a hissing monster.'

'And a sneezing ape.'

'It is a raw meal.'

'No one eats it without setting his throat and stomach ablaze.'

'Everywhere in Bivan's house, people are queuing behind lies and their stomachs. No one is queuing behind the truth and his head.'

'That's very true. People have abandoned their heads and the truth and sided with lies and their stomachs. No one is queuing behind the truth and his head.'

For a while no one spoke. Both of them seemed lost in their own thoughts. But the woman soon recovered herself from her thoughts and said, 'Now that your child has eaten something, perhaps you can leave my house.'

Even before she said it, Talgon knew that was what she was going to say. So he had his requests ready by the time she finished talking.

'Please, can I ask for two more things?'

'Two, not even one. Well, what are these two things you want?' asked the woman with barely concealed impatience.

'Give me a chance to help your husband and allow me and the child a little more time to rest on your veranda.'

'Now I can see you are insane,' said the woman, surprise branded vividly on her face. 'Why should you help my husband? Where do you know him before?'

'He is in pains and needs help from human beings.'

'Of what use will your help be to him? He has already lost his face. If you save his life, will you find a face for him?'

'What ate his face like this?'

'Acid. Students I believe he had wronged took advantage of the religious crisis to hit back at him. They poured acid on him after forcing him to drink a poisonous substance. Lying there, it is not only his face that has been eaten by poison, but his intestines as well.'

'That was very cruel,' Talgon said, feeling very cold inside. 'I can see you have a limmi tree,' he went on after a brief pause. 'The leaves of a limmi tree not only reduce the pains of wounds and make them dry faster, they help a man who has taken poison to vomit it. Please, get some of the leaves for me.'

'It is before you. You may do as you wish. You can't manoeuvre me into helping him – something I have sworn not to.'

'Is this man truly your husband?'

'Yes, he is, but he ill-used me. No one can live with him without running short of love.'

From what Talgon had seen of this woman, if indeed the man on the ground was her husband, he saw little prospects for their marriage now that the man had lost his face. So, from the point of the continuity of their marriage and happiness in it, if it had been happy, there was no point in the man surviving. Without saying anything more to the woman, he went and cut some of the leaves of the limmi tree and pounded the leaves into a pulp in a mortar the woman upon request reluctantly gave him. After pounding the leaves to a pulp, he mixed the pounded pulp with water, sieved out the pulp and took the water to the maimed man, but found him to be still unconscious. Even if he was conscious, he had no mouth to drink the medicinal water. Frustrated, he left the water beside the man and began to apply the pulp on his own wounds. 'Can we carry him inside? It is inhuman to leave him lying there the way he is,' he said to the woman after he had finished applying the pulp on his wounds.

'Like I said before, you can't maneuver me into helping him.'

'Please, have pity.'

To Talgon's shock, the woman began singing a soulful tune he found gripping.

'So, you carry such treasure inside you?' he asked not hiding his surprise.

'I do, but he had no regard for it. There were more ways than one in which my marriage to that man was more than a mistake.'

'Why didn't you get a divorce then?'

'I would have; but he had always threatened me that if ever I leave him, he would hunt me down and pour acid on me and I know he would do so,' she said bitterly. 'No evil thing is beyond him.'

As she spoke, Talgon could feel the heat of her bitterness and hate for the maimed man almost scorching him. Knowing there was nothing he could say to relieve her bitterness, he said nothing.

'When I am this languorous, the only thing that cheers me is music,' the woman said after an interval of silence.

'But you should be happy that harm has befallen your tormentor.'

'I am; but I am not happy that he seemed numbed by the harm that has befallen him. He does not seem to feel the pain he has being inflicting on me.'

Talgon not liking the pain he was seeing on her face decided to indulge her; after all, in her own bitter way, she had not only indulged him, she had helped him and the child. I cannot sing like you, but I can play the *mondo* very well,' he said with some excitement in his voice.

'Is that true?' the woman asked, looking at him with a mixture of excitement and shock. While he could explain the excitement, he could not the shock.

'It's true,' Talgon said.

Using the lantern light, the woman scanned his face. Talgon puzzled by her behavior sat saying nothing. When she seemed to have finished scanning his face, he asked her why she was behaving the way she was.

'I want to assure myself you are not my father,' she said at last, putting down the lantern. 'You seemed to have many things in common. Like you, he loved *mondo* music and played the *mondo* well. In fact, I was brought up on *mondo* music. Inside this house I have one of my father's *mondos* which I am keeping as a heirloom from him. Sometimes I even try playing it the way my father used to, but I simply don't have the talent. I think the talent of playing *mondo* is the exclusive talent of men while that of singing is that of women.'

In his mind Talgon agreed with her and even thought so many other gifts of a woman are in her mouth. 'If indeed you have your father's *mondo* bring it to me and let me try my hands on it,' he said to the woman. 'I only hope I will not disappoint you knowing you are used to good *mondo* music,' he added, seeing the rising excitement in the woman.

'With the delight of a little child, the woman went inside the house and brought a *mondo* and gave it to Talgon.

Talgon ran his fingers on the strings of the *mondo*. He found the strings lax as he had expected. When the *mondo* is not frequently used, the ridges which pull the strings usually slide down making the strings flabby and that was what had happened to the *mondo* the woman gave him. Using both hands, he screwed the ridges back to their proper position and the strings were now taut and resonant when he ran his fingers through them again. He balanced his fingers on the *mondo* and began playing and singing with the expertise of practice:

> Light like a feather
> Happiness gives wings to the limbs of men
> Heavy like a ton of stones
> Sadness plucks wind from the wings of men
> When sadness falls on happiness
> It fractures it
> When happiness falls on sadness
> It merely grazes it
> Sadness fans happiness
> And happiness fans sadness
> Sadness stokes happiness
> And happiness stokes sadness
> An island is never so beautiful
> Until it is surrounded by water
> An oasis is never so taking
> Until it is surrounded by a desert
> A lawn is never so alluring
> Until it is surrounded by a wilderness.

As Talgon sang and played the *mondo*, the woman was getting so entranced that when he stopped playing, she started with the wild expression of one rudely woken up from a pleasant dream.   'Do you believe in destiny?' she asked him, her face flushed with unblemished satisfaction.

'No, I don't.'

'If you believe in destiny, I would have told you it was destiny that brought you to this house at a time like this to give me joy I have not known a long while off,' she said. For the first time she was looking human in Talgon's eyes. 'Seeing you, one will not know you can play the *mondo* so well.'

'I am happy you are pleased with my skills.'

'Who wouldn't, particularly in my circumstances?' she said, giving Talgon a look he could not interpret then but later. 'The music from the *mondo* you just played is sweeter than the music of the wind in the trees in a quiet, windy night. The beat of the *mondo* weaves into my heartbeats so much as to be part of them. It was like you were not playing on the strings of the *mondo*, but on my heartstrings. You seemed to be a wonderful man in many ways. But why don't you believe in destiny?'

By her tone Talgon got the impression his lack of faith in destiny had taken away all she thought was wonderful about him.

'I don't believe in destiny because it introduces order into disorder and design into chance. From what I can see, there is more chance in life than destiny.'

'I believe in destiny because of what I have gone through in my life. I believe in destiny more particularly because of what happened today.'

'What have you gone through in life, and what happened today?'

'Both my life and what happened today are before your eyes.'

'I don't think so. Please, tell me your story.'

'You have asked that you be fed with bitter apples,' said the woman, taking hold of Talgon's hand to lead him into the room. 'This is a long story I can't tell outside with the wind against my face. It must be inside a room with the door closed.' She began pulling him towards the house.

Talgon gently wrested his hand from her grip and picked up the child from where he had laid him. With the child in his arms, he followed the woman into the house.

When they entered the living room, the woman closed the door and went to sit on a chair near the door to a bedroom. Talgon lay the child on a couch she indicated and sat on a chair opposite hers, the palms of his two hands serving as prams to his cheeks. The room impressed him as enjoying the service of a respectable income which he posted to the credit of the man lying outside.

Chapter Seven

Talgon and the woman hardly sat down in the room when they heard the yelping of a dog in front of the house. The dog was apparently in great pain. The woman taking her torch with her leapt up from her seat in great agitation and went to the front door. Talgon sitting where he was watched her wondering why she was so agitated over the yelping of a dog considering her cold attitude to human suffering. When she got to the front door, she opened the door and stood on the doorway, the light of her torch on the dog. After standing by the door for a while, with a trembling hand, she turned and beckoned Talgon. He stood up and walked to her still perplexed by her reaction to the yelping of the dog outside.

The dog in front of the house was a sort of hound that looked well fed despite the fact that it had lost one of its legs and its head had been severely bludgeoned. Standing on three legs, the dog was swinging its bludgeoned head and spilling blood about as it did so.

'That's our dog,' the woman said in a tearful voice. 'Though a beast, it is much kinder to me than the man that calls himself my husband.'

Talgon looking at the dog felt a little sick inside him. 'What do you think happened to it?' he asked, knowing very well the violence that swept through the town that day maimed the dog as it maimed him.

The woman did not say anything probably because she thought he knew the answer to his question. For a while, they stood in silence watching the dog yelping in pain in front of the house. The woman only ran to the dog when it fell to the ground and began snorting in the throes of death. Talgon followed her. But the dog was dead by the time they got to it.

'Poor Nicholas,' the woman wept.

'Was that its name?' Talgon asked.

The woman nodded her head.

'I can see it meant so much to you.'

'It was the only friend I had in this house,' whimpered the woman. 'In fact, it is one of the reasons you met me in this house. I was waiting for its return when you came.'

'Throughout history, the dog has always been a reliable ally.'

'But the man lying there does not have a high opinion of the dog's loyalty to man,' said the woman. 'To him, the dog is friend to man because it knows what the hyena will do to it if man is not standing in front of it. Fearing the tyranny of the hyena, the dog became the colony of man.'

'He might be right. But even in that low opinion of the dog, something good can still be found for it. If the dog can make the smart move your husband talks of, it means it is neither the idiot some people supposed it to be nor the traitor the hyena calls it.'

'This dog meant much more to me than the beast lying there,' the woman said after an interval of silence.

'You mean your husband?'

'My husband,' she muttered and shook her head violently as if to quell a riot going on there. 'Let's go inside,' she said, turning to head back into the house.

Talgon followed her.

Inside, she closed the door behind Talgon before going to sit on the cushion she sat earlier. 'That man is not my husband,' she said as if wanting others to believe he was not her husband as she wanted to convince herself he wasn't.

'What is he to you if he is not your husband?' asked Talgon.

'Wilkim,' murmured the woman.

'What is Wilkim?'

Wilkim is a monster in a folktale my mother told me. This monster took the form of a pleasant gentleman and charmed Jumaim the most beautiful girl in Babuje country to marry him. Several young men had sought the hand of Jumaim in marriage, but she as proud as ever had spurned their love overtures and marriage offers. Her mother seeking to make her take her suitors more seriously always told her that in the beginning many men turn up with flowers seeking the heart of a beautiful girl. But if she turns them away without regard, they would turn up again with flowers like the first time; but the flowers would not be for her heart but for the grave her hopes of marriage were buried. Such a girl would end up a widow not of a dead husband, but of dead expectations of ever getting married. Though always haunted by her mother's counsel, Jumaim seemed incapable of accepting any of her several suitors as husband until Wilkim turned up one morning well dressed and plying good breeding and wholesome manners. Jumaim was in the river fetching water when Wilkim arrived. Words reached her that a suitor was at home seeking to see her. Jumaim sent back word that if the suitor was as handsome as they said, he may wait for her return. But if he wasn't, he needn't waste his time. The reply came to her that the suitor was indeed handsome and would wait. Soon she returned from the river to meet the breath-taking, handsome Wilkim waiting for her outside her father's house. Jumaim was so charmed by the beauty of Wilkim that she would not let him out of her sight again. She wanted an immediate wedding against the caution of her father. She was wedded to Wilkim and she set out with him to the groom's house. They kept boring into the forest like a well digger into the bowels of the earth. Soon Jumaim started getting afraid. 'Is your village buried so deep in the forest?' she asked Wilkim, unable to contain her rising anxiety and fear any longer.

'Will you shut up!' shouted Wilkim who immediately transformed himself into the nine-footed monster he was.

Jumaim on seeing the monster began to run,

crying. The monster ran after her, but before he could lay his claws on her, a tall tree lay down for her to climb. She climbed the tree and the tree stood up with her on top. The monster immediately began chopping the tree with an axe. Jumaim on top of the tree could see her village and even a man going to her father's house. She called on the man to please tell her brothers to come to the forest and rescue her from the monster that wanted to eat her up. The man heard her and ran to her father's house to inform her brothers who soon came out of their house with bows, arrows and spears and headed for the forest where their sister and the monster were.

In the forest, the monster was about felling the tree. A frog in a nearby pond said to the monster, "I can see you are tired of cutting this tree; please, let me help you." The monster gave the axe to the frog who began cutting the tree singing a song that restored the tree to what it was before the monster started felling it. The monster was angry and seized the axe from the frog and began felling the tree again. But soon Jumaim's brothers arrived and fought the monster until they killed it. Jumaim climbed down the tree and was taken home by her brothers.'

'A very interesting story,' said Talgon when the woman came to the end of her story. 'How is your husband Wilkim to you?'

'The man lying out there was not originally

my husband, but my mathematics lecturer. When he was courting me, he was such a kind and generous man that waiting to be married to him was such an agony to me. I allowed him put me in the family way and became his wife. But as soon as we got married, he became a different man. After I packed into his house, he persuaded me to abort the pregnancy saying as a student I could not afford to keep it. I agreed and aborted the pregnancy. Other pregnancies followed which were aborted either because I was still a student or, when that reason was no longer tenable, because he was not ready to father a child. This continued until I could no longer conceive because I had run out of a womb. Then it was too late to leave him. Having become barren who would I marry and hope he would tolerate my barrenness? There was more chance of the man who made me barren putting up with me knowing himself to be responsible for my condition than another man.

'Wilkim seeing I was trapped became desperately wicked. To ensure I got no badun of his, he went to the market and purchased all the foodstuffs needed in the house. He held the keys to the store where the foodstuffs were kept and measured for me such miserable quantity of provender his miserly nature made allowance for. Before my eyes, he flirted with even my friends. When there was no reason for him to beat me, he accused me of seeing other men. Perhaps more torturous to me was his attitude towards my father when he was still alive. In our matrimonial home he called him a simpleton and moron that would believe anything. But whenever he saw him, he was all courtesies and humility that my father would not believe the torment I was going through in his house. When I threatened to leave him, he attempted poisoning me. When he failed to poison me and I appeared bent on leaving him, he threatened to give me an acid bath if I do. He wants to keep me not because he has any use for me, but because he is happy whenever I am unhappy. By various acts of cruelty Wilkim made me fear him the way ancient women feared the masquerade. Whenever I heard him approaching the house, I begin to shrink inside like a little mimosa and to shiver outside like a cold-stricken vagabond. There was no tree I could run and climb and no brother whose help I could call on; and I think I didn't even have the heart to run and climb any tree if one lay to my rescue. Whether because I was paralyzed by my fear of him or because of his diabolism on me, I stayed and bore his terror like a donkey and his humiliations like a dog. But every day I stayed with him only served to make me hate him with an intensity that sometimes made me pant. It was in this situation the religious conflict erupted to reduce him to what is lying there. The acid he wanted to bathe me with, he was the one that eventually was bathed with it. You see why I believe in destiny?'

'It's terrible if indeed he is making you suffer the way you said,' Talgon said, looking at the woman with pity.

'That's how I have been living my life,' the woman said in a voice full of self-pity. When Talgon did not say anything, she said, 'I believe you have been brought to this house by providence to give me happiness I have never known.'

'That will be placing too much value on any happiness I might have brought to you and too much importance on the necessity of your happiness.'

'It is for me who knows my condition to say so.'

'It will be terrible for your husband to die without a face.'

'It would be more terrible for him to live without one.'

'Those who did this to him want to send him to his ancestors in a form they will not like to receive him.'

'He asked for what he got.'

'You hate him so much.'

'I am not Christ to love those that hate me. I am only a poor ill-used woman who loves those that love her and hates those who hate her.' Her voice sounded like that of an old woman pining under the burden of age.

'You are a very bitter person.'

'No one would live with that man without becoming bitter. Thinking of it now, the man has always been without a face. Those who maimed him merely removed the veil over his inhumanness so that the world can see the horror behind the veil.'

Talgon sighed sadly, but did not say anything.

'I don't think there is any man alive in the whole world like that man who knows how to deceive women and make them believe they are everything in his life,' the woman said after an interval of silence. 'He is the sort of man my uncle once told me about. Sitting between his two wives, this man my uncle told me about turned to the one by his right and said, "you know you are the apple of my eyes and that's why you are sitting by my right." She smiled, glowing with pride. Turning to the one by his left, he said, "you know I love you so dearly and that's why you are sitting by my left where my heart is." She too smiled feeling so fulfilled.'

Talgon laughed in spite of himself.

'The father of the man lying out there was that kind of crook,' the woman said after a brief moment of silence. 'He divorced his wife who he wedded in the church. When the pastor who wedded him reminded him of his marital vow of *till death do us part* – a vow he made before God; you wouldn't believe what the rascal told the pastor.'

'What did he tell the pastor?' Talgon asked with a note of eagerness in his voice.

'He said he did not make any such vow before God or anybody because according to him, he was merely reciting the marital vows after the pastor. In other words, it was the pastor that was making the vows, not him.'

Again, Talgon laughed.

Chapter Eight

As a child, Talgon was told that mosquitoes wail round the ears to confirm whether or not their prey is awake or asleep. If he is awake, he would certainly swat at them with his palm. If he does not, it means he is asleep and so they can feast as they like. Sitting on a high-backed chair facing the woman, a mosquito wailed round his ear. 'I am still awake,' he murmured, swatting at the mosquito.

'What did you say?' the woman asked.

'I was only talking to myself,' Talgon said, gnashing his teeth. 'For many people, life in Bivan's house is becoming a nightmare every day,' he continued talking after a momentary pause.

'That's very true,' said the woman. 'The worse thing is that there is no waking up from this nightmare.'

'But your husband is in a humane profession, a profession of service. Why, by your account, should he be what he is?'

'Though a professor of mathematics in the university that man does not see his profession as that of service. For him, it is a business he has to rake in so much money.'

'Bivan's house,' Talgon murmured. 'Even our mathematics professors don't seem capable of working out the simplest arithmetic of how countries that are now prospering got to where they are. And so we are standing on their heads all the values that had propelled other societies to progress and that is why we are damned for all times.'

'That man wants to live like a chief though he is in the profession of those who should despise royalty,' said the woman. 'In fact, he accepted a chieftaincy title in his village after becoming professor of mathematics. He opened a bank account where students who want to pass his course must pay fifty thousand baduns. The sum total of his professorial algebra is not what he knows, but how much money he has.'

'What is the name of your husband?'

'Yagu.'

'Yagu! I see, I see,' Talgon muttered to himself. He had heard so much about Yagu, but never knew him in person. The man was said to be very corrupt and though a professor, he seemed to profess no knowledge or be interested in professing it. He was rather interested in exuding money. Once, he was appointed a commissioner of the national electoral commission. He with other staff of the commission were bribed to return the big feast of Chimla state who everyone knew lost the election because of his unpopularity with the electorates. Now look at what has happened to him. 'But how did we arrive where we are?' he asked of no one.

'We began our journey to where we are when Bajewa our former primehead said morals do not matter in the progress of a society and we agreed. One thing leads to another and here we are where we are.'

'The condition of the life of a man today is the child of the choices he made yesterday.'

'As you make your bed so shall you lie on it.'

'Corruption and leprosy are cousins. Just by a handshake you can contract leprosy. It is the same thing with corruption. Corruption corrupts the mind, leprosy the body. Like leprosy corruption seems to be a tropical disease. Though easy to contract, both corruption and leprosy are difficult to cure. Even when cured, if any of these diseases has already eaten up your fingers, you go to the grave with the stigma. In this sense corruption and leprosy are incurable.'

'Your analogy fits the matter like horns on the devil's head and a tail in his ass.'

'It is sad that the only measure of value in this country is money,' Talgon said in an emotional voice. 'Instead of lecturers seeing themselves as wheelers of knowledge and apostles of right, they see themselves as merchants of money while society sees them as abettors of fraud. It is sad.'

'Everyone in this country has been reduced to an economic measure,' said the woman. 'The pressure of the many things we now have to eat has ensured that. Look at university students. They no longer read. Learning stops at the secondary school. University students no longer attend classes. Instead, they go into town and hustle for money to give their lecturers to pass them. At the secondary school where students are too young to hustle, the teachers teach little because they know little. They know little because they were taught little while in the university. Because their salaries cannot feed them and their families, they too have to hustle. Everyone is hustling, but no one is getting anywhere. Our situation is such that anyone can be a victim of anything any moment. Some people were victims of the man lying there. He in the end fell victim to others.'

'We are not living life, but faking it,' said Talgon with a forlorn look on his face. 'A friend told me that for him to be granted access into Jonka Palace by the police at the gate, he had to roll up the glasses of his car that has no air conditioner. Seeing he was a big man, the police quickly opened the gate for him. Somewhere inside the sweeping premises of the palace, he had to park and rush out of the boiling heat inside the car. Everyone wants to be seen as a big man and so the poor have contempt for themselves.'

'Everyone wants to be rich by hook or crook because everything has to be paid for,' said the woman, languorously. 'All it takes to be recruited into the police force is fifty thousand baduns paid to police headquarters and you are recruited. A week ago, some armed robbers caught in Binchi, under torture by the police, told the police some members of their gang were being trained as recruits in the police college at Binchi. No doubt, they got recruited because they were able to pay their way through. By getting recruited into the police force, they had become licensed criminals.'

'What you 'just said reminds me of the police corporal who some years ago was living big,' Talgon said in a sad tone. 'No one knew he was living big because he was stealing and selling electric cables leading to villages and small towns electric poles and cables had been taken, but were yet to get power. As a rich man, inspectors were answering *sir* to him because he had more money than them.'

'No one gets promoted in the police force unless he has been making returns to headquarters. This way junior police officers get promoted over their seniors,' the woman said, waving her hand in a worldly manner only men were known to. 'Please, play the *mondo* again for me. All this talk about Bivan's house is beginning to make me very sad.'

'I suffer your condition too,' said Talgon. 'Often talking about Bivan's house or even news about it makes me hypertensive. Talking about the country or news about it are to me what salt is to a hypertensive patient. The *mondo* is the exercise or rest that gives me back my wellbeing. Humming a tune, he began playing the *mondo* again, a bemused expression bestriding his face. In the ears of the woman the *mondo* was more melodious now than the first time he played it. Once more he was a wonderful man despite his lack of faith in destiny.

'I feel so happy having you in my house. The melody from your *mondo* has pumped a lot of life into me,' said the woman when Talgon stopped playing the *mondo*. There was warmth in her voice that leaned out to embrace him.

'I am happy to be of service to you.'

'What is the tune you just played on the *mondo* saying?'

'It is saying:

Happiness is a guest; sadness is the host
Comedy is a guest; tragedy is the host
The host of life keeps
Rushing the guest out of doors
And there is no inn for the guest to go to
Tragedy and injustice – the two threads of life
Are stitching their tattered cloth
Into a messy, poor thing
My eyes cannot look upon
I have no lips for the songs of life
But I have ears for the wailings of life
Life petty, lowly and lonely
Frivolous, empty and desperate
Waddles on to neither point nor good.

'Not a surprising song from someone who does not believe in destiny,' the woman said, looking fondly at Talgon. 'But I would have thought a song like this would be salt to a hypertensive.'

'It is man-made miseries that make me hypertensive not miseries life is heir to. Even if the words of this song were liable to make me hypertensive, the exercise and rest in the *mondo* will relieve the sting.'

'I hold your pipe there,' said the woman full of verve. 'You played two tunes on the *mondo*, what is the song for the second tune?'

> Time feeds on the thorns of the roses
> As on the filament of the hedged roses
> The thorns can neither bar it with their pricks
> Nor the roses tame it with their beauty
> Time feeds on the air and bodies of the sky
> As on the dust and water of the earth
> There is no termite like time
> It eats up a man before eating up his footprints
> Everything and anything perishes with time
> There is no eternity on earth or in the sky
> For man, spirit or even the rock and dust
> Whoever thinks of the cruelty of time
> Would not work for a name.

'What a song from a man who looks so kindly upon life!' exclaimed the woman. 'If you think time washes away the footprints of a man, why are you leaving footprints of kindness on your path?'

'Perhaps to give time something to eat before it moves on to claim its next victim. Perhaps to live with myself.'

'I find this song you just sang as touching as the first rain of the rainy season and true of life as balls of dung are true of the dung beetle,' said the woman in an abject tone. 'Everything decays and withers away with time leaving no trace that it was once there. The unfortunate thing is that people decay much faster than other things. Trees, for example, do not decay as fast as people. Depending on the nature of a person's genetic build-up, his or her attitude to life, his or her economic condition, he or she decays faster or slower. But we all decay. People in comfortable economic conditions decay slower. To me such people are like refrigerated tomatoes or meat. They decay slowly because of the preservation of the refrigerator. But once their economic condition changes from good to bad, they begin to decay faster. There is power outage and the fridge is no longer working. So the tomatoes or meat in the fridge begins to rot faster.

'I have sung this song several times on the *mondo*, but do you know I have never conjured up these graphic images you just conjured?' Talgon said, marveling at the woman.

'It is a common human disability that we don't often see things under our noses,' said the woman, looking at Talgon affectionately. 'You see, I am not interested in people,' she continued in a voice full of heart-melting charm. 'But you are different. You are more spiritual than human.'

'I am all too human. But I am not happy to hear you say you are not interested in people. You are human and people need people,' said Talgon. 'You have ears not to hear what you say to yourself, but what others say to you. For that matter, your mouth is not for talking to yourself, but to others. You can see that as hearing and talking organs, your ears and mouth will not be of much use to you without people. Life is all about selling or buying something. You are either selling or buying an idea, a story, a commodity, a courtesy like an exchange of greetings in the morning, or even a rumor, a gossip or a lie. You can neither sell nor buy any of these things from yourself; and without selling or buying these things, you can't be happy. People need people to be happy.'

'If you are all human as you said, I might be interested in people for the first time in my life.'

'I am all human alright,' Talgon said with an infectious air of fellowship. 'You see the reason why our world is sick and dying today is because people have lost interest in people. People steal public money because they have no interest in people. If you love something, you will not like it to suffer. If we can find interest in people again, we will recover from our sickness.'

'You have to pass the night here,' said the woman with such grace and lure that Talgon found difficult to resist.

'On account of my leg and the child who I may not

be able to carry feeling the way I am, I would not say no,'
he said.

'There is a spare bedroom you can use,' said the
woman.

'That would not be right,' said Talgon in a firm voice.
'I am a stranger and it is not proper to sleep inside another
man's house with his wife sleeping inside the same house
with the husband absent.'

'But Wilkim is not absent,' said the woman, wistfully.

'And he is not present either.'

'He is the one lying out there.'

'I have no doubt. But he is as good as absent. We will
take your husband in while I sleep out there on the
veranda. Hear me talking of sleep. This is not a night of
sleep for me. I will stay there on the veranda and speak to
the world with the *mondo*.'

'I will not be happy if you stay outside. Like I said,
there is a spare bedroom you can use.'

'I feel sad to make you unhappy. But it's not right
madam. Let me help you carry your husband in.'

'My husband.' It was a near inaudible murmur, but
Talgon heard it. What alarmed him was the distaste that
ran through those two words. He stood up and walked out
of the house to where the man was lying. Already his leg
was not aching him like before. It seemed the herb was
already taking effect.

The woman followed him only as far as the veranda
of the house. Standing on the veranda, she said, 'since you
so much care for him, leave him out there. The cold
outside is more likely to wake him up than the warm

inside.'

What the woman said made sense to Talgon. When a person faints, it is cold water that is poured on him to revive him. He walked back to where the woman was sitting. 'Bivan's house,' he sighed and yawned.

'The house of greed,' said the woman.

'On every horse a bridle is cast or it runs amok,' said Talgon, his eyes in the direction of the maimed man. 'Greed is an unruly horse. The bridle on it is people's contempt for it. It is not for nothing the devil will be cast into the bottomless pit. It is out of fear that if left roaming about the nether regions he would wreck mischief in heaven. So, he is chained by the bottomless pit. The beast in man called greed must be chained by people's disdain of it. But, in Bivan's house, this beast is left to roam without a rein of any kind. So, everyone might express his greed anyway he likes without the fear of the sanction of contempt.'

'With pride, a poor man in Bivan's house who is a victim of a rich man who stole public money calls the rich man his brother.'

'What you just said reminds me of a Christmas ceremony I attended recently. A wealthy woman politician holding political office who everyone knows is a prostitute was made *the Mother of the Day* by the organizers of the ceremony and everyone at the ceremony was happy to have a prostitute as a mother.'

'Rather than chain greed in a bottomless pit,

greed in Bivan's house is the bottomless pit that swallows everyone and everything.'

'Almost everyone you see in this house is a walking fraud. 'Everyone you see is a smiling dupe; but the whole nation is a frowning mess.' Saying this, Talgon began playing the *mondo* again:

Little glow worms flaring in the swamp at night
    One dies, another comes alive in a chore
    That sucks and wastes the sap of life
    Meteors twinkling out of darkness
    And melting into caves of the air
    Finding life a wretch he cannot live with
    He embraced death a hole he would not know.

'The words of the song are as moving as the tune so much that one can say the poetry of the song sounds through the tune,' said the woman, a look of utter satisfaction on her face. 'But I hope this song has nothing to do with Wilkim,' she said after a momentary pause; 'because in his case, if he found life a wretch, life must have found him a leech long before he found it a wretch.'

'The song has nothing to do with your husband,' said Talgon, impressed by the woman's wits. 'It is an old song my father used to sing to me. A man fed up with the drudgery and humdrum of life committed suicide. Years after his death, the women of his village composed on him the song I just sang.'

A meteor flashed across the sky.

'Someone said meteors are sparks from the fire of hell,' said the woman.

'I will rather think, they are sparks from the volcanoes of the air,' Talgon said.

Chapter Nine

Five houses away from the house Talgon was playing the *mondo*, a horse dismembered by the rampaging fanatics lay grunting in pain. The owner of the horse laid a few metres away from his horse with a broken leg. His wife and two children he did not know where they were or what had happened to them. They were not at home when the religious war erupted. Since its eruption he had not seen them. Like Talgon, he had seen the burning lantern in the house Talgon was and wanted to go and seek help for himself, but his broken leg would not allow him. His throat was so choky and sore from the smoke of burning tyres and houses he had inhaled that he could not even cry loudly for help. He could only whimper on the ground where he lay. He began crawling towards the lantern about the same time Talgon decided to head for it. All the while Talgon has been in the house, he has been crawling towards it. When Talgon first began playing the *mondo*, the pain in his leg seemed to abate and he felt light, almost giddy in the head. But instead of using the abatement in pain to crawl faster towards the house, he stopped crawling to absorb the music. It was only when Talgon stopped playing the *mondo* that he started crawling painfully once more towards the house. Now that Talgon was playing the soulful instrument again, he had stopped crawling again to listen. But now he was no longer far from the house. Even with his sore throat, he could whimper where he was now and be heard in the house.

When Talgon stopped playing the *mondo*, the wounded man cried out for help with all the remaining strength in him. The woman was with Talgon on the veranda where he was playing the musical instrument. She was looking at him with admiration and a longing his character would not allow him see. Talgon on hearing the cry of the man which was more of a groan of pain than a cry for help, stood up to go and help.

'Where are you going?' asked the woman, taking hold of him.

'You heard the cry. Someone is in pains and needs help.'

'I am in pains too and need help.'

'But you are well. You are not sick. Please, let me go and help whoever it is.'

'It is not the type of sickness you have in mind that I am talking about. The moment you played that *mondo,* my heart left me and went to you. It is yet to return to me.'

'You can't be serious,' said Talgon with a sinking feeling.

'No one has ever been more serious.'

'You have a husband and he is lying there critically sick,' Talgon feeling suddenly alarmed, sought to take her mind from him to her husband.

'He will not make it,' said the woman in a voice full of shocking certitude. 'Even if he makes it, it is over between us.'

Talgon's heart was beating faster now. For a long while he was silent.

'Contrasting him with you makes me hate him more.'

'You barely know me,' Talgon said, trying to pull the woman from her impulsive inclination that was beginning to frighten him. 'I may not be shining inside as I seem to you to shine outside.'

'As for not knowing you, that's where you are wrong. It does not take long to know honest and compassionate people like you. The windows and door of your heart are open like a parachute. Through the windows I can see what is in your heart, but there is a net at the door preventing me from entering. Like I said, you are just like my father and you can't say I didn't know my father. I will like to die with the soundtracks of your music directing my footsteps to heaven.'

The cry of the injured man crawling towards the house came to them again, in the ears of Talgon, more pathetic than the first time; in the ears of the woman, more irritating than before. He wrested his hand from her grip and limped towards the source of the cry. The woman ran after him, trying to clutch at him with her outstretched hands which he kept brushing off. 'Remember you can't bring anyone into this house because it's not your house,' she protested in a whining, feverish voice.

'I know that very well,' said Talgon. 'I want to see if I can help him where he is and take him to his house if I can. After I will come and fetch that poor child. I am really grateful for your kindness of heart in giving him food and a bed to lie on.'

'I am sorry to speak thus to you,' said the woman in tears. 'I do not mean to drive you from my house. Please, don't go; don't leave me alone.'

The woman that was hard and cold like ice has now melted into water. Talgon could not understand any of it. He did not say anything and in fact could not say anything.

Talgon with the woman behind him found the man with the broken leg in a ditch he was finding difficult to crawl out of. He was all bathed in sweat, blood and dust. 'Please, help me; I am dying,' he said in a whining, tattered voice. He was lying on his side, his head supported by his left hand, his face turned up towards Talgon and the woman, his eyes looking sightlessly at them. Talgon took hold of his right hand. Using the torchlight the woman brought with her, he examined the palm of the wounded man. 'The palm is white and pale,' he said after his examination. 'It appears he has lost so much blood and needs blood transfusion urgently or he would die.'

'Where will you get blood to give him?' asked the woman, her hands folded on her breasts, her mind not in the least disposition to find help for the dying man, but rather full of anger for his interruption of intimate feelings she had sprung upon Talgon so artfully.

'Please, help me,' cried the man in a much weaker voice. The strain of supporting his head with his right hand proved too much for his hand and it collapsed under his head. He fell back on his back and his right hand held loosely by Talgon was flung out of hold to lie lifelessly several inches wide of his body.

'He is dying,' cried Talgon.

'What is he waiting for?' said the woman in a voice that carried a sword.

In all his life, Talgon had never heard anything said with such callous indifference. 'Where is your heart?'

'It is with you.'

'That's not true. Your heart can't live near mine and you speak the way you do.'

Does this mean he would not mind my heart being near his if only my heart will be like his? wondered the woman, pleasurably. Is it a trick for me to help? No, people like him are incapable of tricks. There is hope. 'What do you want me to do for us to help him?' she asked in a soft, pleasant voice. She stepped out behind him and stood beside him.

With a puzzled expression on his face, Talgon looked at her sharply. 'We can't carry him far,' he said. 'We have to get a vehicle to carry him to the hospital.'

'There is no vehicle on the road,' the woman

reminded him.

'I have almost forgotten about that. This is bad,' said Talgon at the end of his wits. He looked at the injured man on the ground. He was no longer gasping. He shook him, but the man did not stir. He was dead. 'He is dead,' he murmured what they both knew.

'He no longer needs the hospital and we no longer need a vehicle,' said the woman. 'Death has a miraculous way of solving all problems.'

Talgon did not immediately say anything probably because he thought there was truth in what the woman said, cruel as he thought it was. 'But he has to be buried,' he said at last.

'Buried?' the woman chuckled, mirthlessly. 'How many people are you going to bury tonight or the day after?'

Talgon did not say anything. The woman had again spoken the searing truth he had come to associate with her. At the wedding reception venue, he had walked away from many corpses, how many was he able to bury? He shook his head sadly, turned and walked away from the dead man. The woman and her truth walked behind him.

'I wish you can see some things the way I do,' Talgon said as they neared the house.

'As I said before,' the woman returned, wistfully, 'there are many ways in which you resembled my father. I have my eyes, but my father insisted I use his. I was to live in his womb forever. It is the same with you.'

Talking about eyes reminded Talgon of the woman's husband lying on the ground without eyes. Followed by the woman, he walked to the maimed man to see if he had regained consciousness. 'He is dead,' he said to the woman after touching the injured man.

'Now he is dead and I am alive,' said the woman with the cheerful air of triumph. 'That he tried to poison me but failed is due to destiny. That he should die before me is also destiny.'

Talgon first nodded his head then shook his head.

Chapter Ten

In the neighborhood Talgon grew up, there was an imbecile who slobbered and was incapable of intelligible speech. He could not go to school because he was incapable of learning. He was so despised by his parents that he had neither clothes to wear nor food to eat. He wandered about the neighborhood uncared for and spurned by everyone. He was later found dead in a river he had apparently wandered into and was drowned. The miserable life of this imbecile and his tragic end made Talgon not to believe in destiny. Destiny would mean there is a designer who designed the life of this imbecile to be what it was. Which designer would be so cruel? Even if the imbecile was being punished for his sins in an earlier life, Talgon found the punishment excessive and wicked. Whichever way he looked at the matter, he could not understand why anyone would be destined to be born an imbecile only to wander about like an animal and die without any chance against life. But chaos and accidents could throw up such a person and situation. After all, he had seen wild storms tore away the roof of houses and vehicles running over people only because they happened to be on the path of these disasters. Daily, he saw people encountering one misfortune or the other, enjoying one advantage or the other merely because they happened to be around when misfortune or fortune was passing by. The religious mayhem that took place during the wedding reception was not destiny, but a fortuitous occurrence he and others who attended the wedding reception happened to be around when it happened. He was now in the woman's house not because he was destined to be there, but because chance dictated he be there. The child he rescued from the wedding reception area had a good chance of him being around to help him. Now the woman's husband was dead. The woman had the good fortune of him being around to help her stand the horror.

With the woman's husband now dead, Talgon knew he could no longer leave the house as he had earlier said. He thought it would be unkind to leave her alone with the corpse for the whole night. For a while, he stood looking vacantly at the ground wondering the type of marriage that had existed between the man and his wife. 'What do we do with his body?' he asked the woman, moments later.

'That's what I have being thinking about,' said the woman, licking her lips that seemed so much in need of moisture. For a while none of them spoke. They both seemed at a loss of what to do. There was no mortuary nearby and sleeping in the same house with a corpse was something Talgon did not like and it seemed the woman would even like less. 'Well, there is nothing to be done except to sleep with the corpse till tomorrow,' Talgon said at last.

'There is always something that can be done about any situation. But our fears and hypocrisy always prevent us from doing it.'

'What can we do about this situation except wait till morning?' asked Talgon.

'My fears and hypocrisy will not allow me express it with my mouth, less wrought it with my hands.'

Talgon did not press the question. He walked away from the corpse where he and the woman were standing towards the veranda of the house. The woman followed him like a *Fantam* wife would her husband.

'Where has he gone to?' asked the woman when they were both sitting on the veranda.

'You mean your husband?'

The woman nodded her head.

'That's the mystery of death we are not permitted to know,' said Talgon. 'If we know, we may all follow him and that will be the end of this life.'

'You mean we will all want to die?'

'Yes, we may all want to die. Even without knowing what lies beyond this world, now and then you feel like reaching for a rope and heading for a tree.'

'Do you know the *mondo* you play gives life?' asked the woman, reaching for the *mondo* lying on the ground.

'It could not give life to your husband. He is dead.'

'Even the wind cannot inflate a ruptured balloon,' said the woman with haunting sarcasm. 'Give life to me. I am beginning to run short of it. Please, play the *mondo* for me.' She handed the mondo to Talgon.

He collected the mondo from her, but did not play it.

'Please, play for me,' the woman said when she saw he was unwilling to play the *mondo*.

'No, I will not play it. I don't like its effect on you. It makes you say things you shouldn't.'

'You don't have to play it. You can play my heart. Like I said the beat of the *mondo* is the beat of my heart and its strings my heartstrings. Please, play me,' she said, moving her hands to embrace Talgon by the neck. 'Life is running out on me.'

Talgon tried pulling away from her, but was a little late. Her naked hands wrapped round his neck in a way he thought too artful for a married woman. The feel of her flesh on his neck was sensual and overpowering, but he steeled himself against the persuasion of the feeling and pulled away from her. Realizing it was only the music of the *mondo* that would keep the woman away from him, he began playing the melodious instrument again.

More than the first tune he played, this tune was like a massage on the fluttering nerves of a careworn body. When he stopped playing, the woman in a flash encircled him in her arms. The feel of her supple body against his arouse feelings in him he was soon ashamed of. This is evil he thought. The woman's husband was lying out there dead and here he was on the veranda, in the full glare of the unhappy sky almost swooning in the pleasure of the wife's embrace. It is wicked. He ought to be conscionable than this. So as not to offend the woman, he began pulling away from her gradually until he was completely out of her embrace. Out of the woman's grasp, he began playing the *mondo* again:

The frog is squatting on his hinges
And you are asking him to give you a chair to sit on
The monkey's buttocks are bare
And you are asking him to give you trousers to wear
The skunk is choking from his odor
And you are asking him to give you perfume to wear
The hen is swallowing pebbles without chewing them
And you are asking her to give you teeth to chew your meat.
Do not ask life to give you what it does not have
And you will not be disappointed with what

you get from it.

'Like the others, this song is also true of life,' said the woman. 'Whoever ask life to give him what it does not have is not fair to it. I can even say he is not fair to himself.'

'Like other comments you made on my songs, I find this comment a good exposition of this song,' said Talgon with a lot of admiration for the woman's commonsense.

For a while no one spoke. Talgon finding the silence more pressing said, 'seeing a man on the street or in his house, who will think he can express himself so violently like he did today.'

'You can only speak for yourself,' said the woman. 'For me, a man by his very appearance tells me to beware.'

'How come you are unscathed by the violence that swept through this town?' Talgon asked the woman a question he felt he should have asked much earlier.

'As they say every bullet has its billet.'

'You seem to believe so much in design.'

'Yes, I do. Apart from the *mondo*, it is the only thing that makes sense to me in life.'

'I believe in luck. Between life and death, all I see is luck.'

'Are you an atheist then?'

'No, I believe in luck. In fact, I pray to luck every day. Where were you when it happened?'

'I was with the monkey on my back. I mean I was with Wilkim in this house. I was in my trap.'

'It's sad hearing what is meant to be a blissful consortium turned into a trap for one of the consorts.'

'Only that my own trap was tighter, there are very few marriages I know of that are not traps. But people put up with their traps with the little cheer they can have in a trap. People tolerate their traps merely to meet the demands of society on them.'

'Well, the whole life for that matter is a trap for all of us. We all agree to live in this trap to meet the demands of our fears of the unknown,' said Talgon in a doleful tone, his eyes scanning the skies.

'For some of us there is no doubt that life is a trap. But for someone like you, life clearly is a cheerful song. The melody of the *mondo* breaks the chains of life and makes it float in the air of freedom. It's for people like us that life is a trap.'

Someone grunted. They both looked in the direction of the grunt. It was the woman's husband hobbling towards them.

Chapter Eleven

The Kiyak tribe of Bivan's house was believed to have magical powers it used to walk people who had just died to the forest they would be buried instead of carrying them on the raffia stretch they would be buried in. When Talgon saw the woman's husband he thought was dead shambling towards them, he was possessed by thoughts of Kiyak funeral magic. He sat looking at the man lumbering towards them in the weirdest and most gruesome manner he had never seen or thought of, his mind in a whirlpool of fear and shock. The woman sitting by his side heaved a sigh of fear and passed out. In the mind of Talgon and the woman before she passed out, it was not the man plodding towards them, but his ghost. The man as far they were concerned was dead. When the man came within meters of Talgon, the paralysis holding him to his seat thawed. He jumped up and began backing away from the sightless man. It was then he knew the woman had passed out. He saw her sprawled on the ground beside him, her face awake with the fear that made her faint. She had fallen to the ground without him hearing her thud.

The man kept moving sightlessly without a face, with an eye hanging out, one of his hands thrust out as if it were the walking stick of a blind man feeling the path before him. If the eye hanging from its socket could see, it did not see the body of his wife on his path. He stumbled on her body and fell down with a ghostly thud. For a while his body lay on top of her before rolling onto the floor to lie beside her.

Talgon stood looking at the body on the floor, dizziness and nausea mounting in him. Where the man's face used to be was turned towards the wife; where his mouth used to be slightly parted as if he was saying something to the wife who hard of hearing had tilted her head to one side to hear what he was saying. They lay like that for a while before the man began to cough. Apart from his grunting, it was the first sound to come from him and the house since he appeared to terrify him and the woman. Two clots of blood fell from his mouth when he coughed. After coughing for some time, he lay still and the house was once more engulfed in a disquieting silence. To Talgon, the man was finally dead. Sometime after he lay quiet, his wife lying beside him stirred and gradually opened her eyes. When she saw the body of her husband lying beside her, she screamed and rolled away from the body. Talgon ran to her and helped her to her feet. Holding her by her hand he lugged her away from her husband's body towards the room. Her breath was coming out in short shallow gasp like a broken wind and a ghost-like weird expression kept sliding in and out of her face.

Talgon led her into the room and sat her on a

cushion chair. Sitting on the chair, the woman kept casting frightened glances around her. She was as jumpy as a cat on hot bricks and as out of nerves as a broken reed.

Talgon sitting a chair away from her looked at her with pity in his heart. One moment he was happy he had come to the house and was of help to the woman, another moment he was full of misgivings of the good of his coming. The woman had taken to him in a big way and if he was to be honest with himself, he had feelings for her that were not strangers to hers for him. He could see he had touched her off and she was hanging loose and he could feel her touching him off and he could hang loose as she was if he did not take care. If there was any difference in their mutual affections, it was that his was tempered by discretion while hers had no rein on it. Her condition was such that if she were a man, he would have been sitting by her to soothe her to a better state of nerves. As if she was reading his mind, as soon as this thought came into his mind, she said, 'please come and sit by me. I am feeling very feverish.'

Talgon's heart sank. 'That's not proper,' he said.

'I am sick. Do you want me to die?' moaned the woman

'No.'

'Then come and sit by me.'

He stood up and walked towards her without

much resolution. When he got to where she was sitting, he stood looking at her, strings of sympathy twitching his heart. She looked so ill he was surprised she could remain propped up on her seat.

'Please, sit by me and hold me,' she pleaded, her lips quavering.

He sat down and placed his right hand lamely on her shoulder.

She leaned against him and he had to pass his hand round her abdomen to give her the kind of comfort she needed.

'Providence brought you to save me,' she murmured. If you hadn't come, I would have died.'

'No, you wouldn't have died,' said Talgon. 'But I know what would have happened.'

'What would have happened?'

'You would have run away from this place.'

'Not only with my legs, but with my hands,' said the woman looking up at Talgon longingly. 'You have a pure heart. That's what is eating me up.'

Talgon was about saying something when the little boy he brought to the house with him cried. He cried only once and was quiet again.

'He must be having nightmares,' said the woman.

'Very likely,' said Talgon. I ...'

'No evil spirit is trying to throttle him to death if that's your fear.'

'You have such a quick mind.'

'And such a possessive heart,' said the woman. 'The night has been such a dreadful one for everyone, more so for a child. Apart from what the child went through in the mayhem, this night is full of mares neighing and howling. Such neighs can torment a child as much as any nightmare.'

'You are right about the neighing horses,' said Talgon. 'Many mares must have lost their limbs and spouses to the fire of the fanatics. In the great lamentation of all living creatures this sorrowful night, I have heard the neighing of mares more than the cry of any other suffering creature.'

'The only time they stopped neighing was when you played the *mondo*,' said the woman.

'Are you sure they stopped neighing or the melody of the *mondo* so filled your ears that you could not hear the neighing horses?' said Talgon, knitting his brow into a farm of tiny ridges.

'I hope you are not under any oath to deny yourself any due that is yours,' said the woman. 'Beside me, the horses know the good you do them any time you play the *mondo*. Please, minister once more to me and the horses out there neighing for relief.'

'You know of all creatures, a horse has about the worse voice,' said Talgon. 'So it may not be surprising if more than other creatures, it cherishes good music.' Saying this, he picked the *mondo* and began playing a soulful tune on it. The woman fell back on her chair, placed her hand on her chest and shut her eyes. When he was through, she slowly opened her eyes and asked, 'What was this tune saying?'

'It was saying we should expect little from life and the little we get will please us. That all living creatures should look beyond the fog over their heads to the nightglow of the stars and see the days of peace and happiness that are coming.'

'Nightglows, glow worms; my nightglow is beside me.'

Talgon did not say anything.

'You don't seem to carry a cell phone with you,' the woman said suddenly, her eyes running over Talgon.

'I forgot it at home when I was going to the wedding,' he said.

'No wonder,' she said. 'Since you have been here, no one has called you and you have called no one.'

'Even if I have it with me, it's unlikely anyone would have called me unless my wife who would be wondering what has happened to me; that's if nothing has happened to her. I have little use for the toy if you must know.'

Talgon observed that the woman cringed when he mentioned his wife. For a while her face was clouded by a sad expression that upset her facial symmetry. Feeling her way a little awkwardly to pleasant thoughts, she began to speak after a long silence. 'That makes two of us.

Our lives seemed to be melting into each other on all the edges. All the same, can I have your phone number?'

Talgon gave her his phone number.

'Your name.'

'Talgon.'

'Your own name.'

'Beckin.'

For a while they sat staring at each other no one saying anything. Around them there was quiet. Then the horses began neighing again followed by the shrieking of insects and the braying of donkeys. The ugly music of that night was back again.

'I wish the only sound there is in life is the melody of a *mondo*,' said Beckin.

'You will no longer like it in that case,' said Talgon. 'The cooing of the dove sounds melodious because of the hooting of the owl.' Saying this, he stood up and began limping out of the room.

'Where are you going?' Beckin asked.

'I want to look into the sky and see what is living there now.'

'I hope you are not trying to run away from me?'

'The child I brought is in your room,' said Talgon

'Oh, the poor child,' murmured Beckin.

Outside, Talgon first scanned the sky and was sad to see the nightglow he so much enjoyed viewing was not out this night. Perhaps the madness of humans that day had chilled it in doors. Finding no joy in the sky, he walked to where the body of Beckin's husband was. But when he got there, all he saw was the blood the man vomited. The man was gone.

'What!' cried Talgon.

Chapter Twelve

Talgon had an uncle who lived in a village not far away from Bangora. He was a huge strong man who performed feats no other man in the village could. During festivities, he blew a trumpet other men could produce no sound with. He climbed trees no man could and no one in the village could wrestle with him. In addition to his physical strength, he was a medicine man reputed to have the power to disappear when confronted by danger his great strength could not overcome. Once he was said to have climbed a tree whose stem swelled under him, making it impossible for him to climb down. He sent the man he was in the forest with on an errand only for the man to find him on the ground hale and hearty on his return. Talgon has never believed the strange tales he was told about his uncle. But what he was going through this night with Beckin's husband was beginning to make him wonder if such tales were true after all. For a second time he cried, 'What is this?'

Beckin in the room on hearing Talgon's cries ran out of her room to know what was amiss.

'Your husband's body; it's gone!'

Beckin looked at where her husband's body laid moments ago and to her shock the body was gone. She caught her breath petrified beyond words.

'Impossible!' cried Talgon. 'Who could have carried his corpse?'

'You are talking of his corpse,' said Beckin when she got her breath back. 'I am not sure he was dead in the first place. Maybe he only swooned and the melody of the *mondo* revived him. Even if he had died, it is not beyond Yagu to come back to life if he wished. He is a sorcerer if you don't know. He is Wilkim I told you.'

'There is in what I have seen so far evidence to support what you are saying,' said Talgon. 'It is so mystifying and shocking. The only parallel I can find in history to what I am witnessing tonight were the four deaths of Rasputin Debauche in one night. It is so awesome. May be each time he dies and gets to heaven, he finds the gate of heaven locked against him and he would return to earth. Looking the way he was without a face, he would no doubt find the gate of heaven locked against him.'

'If the gate of heaven is locked against him, he should try the gates of hell. I am sure the gates of hell will be widely opened for him. In fact, the devil himself is sure to be at the main gate to receive him.'

'Rather than go to hell, he prefers here. I believe that's why he keeps returning.'

'Well, he is not welcome here. So he had better go back there. The devil is sure to take pity on him having served him so well on earth. But if the devil fearing he may outshine him in hell bars his way into the infernal regions, outside heaven and hell, the nether regions are full of spirits rejected by both heaven and hell. He should join the spirits roaming the wilds of the nether regions without a home.'

Talgon in deep thought said nothing.

'Ah...I should have seen this possibility. Ah...' cried Beckin. 'I should have cut off his head from his neck to make his resurrection impossible and end my torment in his hands.'

'What are you saying?' asked Talgon aghast. 'Why should you cut off the head of your husband?'

'I will cut off his tongue if I can reach it.'

'Are you out of your mind?'

'All the time I have been talking to you, I have been out of my mind. It's now, I am in my mind,' Beckin said in an even voice.

'Where am I?' cried Talgon, retreating from Beckin in fear.

'You are by a woman in her mind,' said Beckin. 'You have heard my story. You should understand why I am what I am.'

'Whatever you ...'

The cry of the child sleeping in the room came to them again.

'Something evil must be happening to that child in his sleep,' said Talgon, moving towards the house.

Beckin followed him. 'You are the tree that will save me from Wilkim this night and I cannot let you out of my sight.'

'This poor child must have carried those fanatics in the wedding arena who wanted to kill him to his sleep,' said Talgon.

'For me, I will not say so,' said Beckin. 'I will rather

say those who could not kill the poor child in the wedding arena must be attacking him in his sleep. I believe that when I am having a bad dream, either a witch is in the room l am sleeping or demons have entered it.'

They found the child sleeping peacefully once more. Talgon sat on one end of the couch and passed his hand under the child to cuddle him. Beckin sat close to him and leaned away from the darkness to her right as if a hand from the darkness was reaching out for her.

'You are much like this child,' said Talgon. 'You carry in your mind many horrid images of what you have just gone through.'

'You are right there,' said Beckin. 'Because of that I will not let you out of my sight tonight.'

The various times Talgon and Yagu's wife thought Yagu was dead, he had merely fainted. While Talgon and his wife were inside the house, he had come to again, staggered to his feet and began to blunder about not knowing where he was going. He was soon on the deserted street in front of his house. Encountering no obstacles on the street, he blundered along sightlessly not knowing where he was going. He was a frightful sight to behold; mercifully there was no one to behold him. Without a face, drenched in blood and lopping in his walk, he was a bloodcurdling and chilling spectacle. Occasionally a whimper of pain came from where his mouth used to be. It was one of these whimpers that made a victim of the religious mayhem lying in a gutter unable to walk to look to the street. What he saw brought his heart to a standstill. Yagu looked like a resurrected corpse in a horror movie out to petrify. Only that the man in the gutter knew he was not watching a horror movie, but staring at naked reality walking the street without pity. He was looking at what believers in God in Bivan's house could do to show their love for God. 'Bivan's house!' he cried and passed out.

Yagu did not walk far away from the man in the gutter before he stumbled and fell on a bonfire kindled by the fanatics on the street. In Bivan's house, both anger and happiness were celebrated with bonfires on the streets. If the country won a football tournament which was about the only occasion of national happiness in the country, the event was celebrated with bonfires on the streets. If a religious riot broke out which was only one of many conflicts in the country, bonfires were set up on the streets to celebrate anger. The bonfires were always set up with discarded tyres and any wastes the youths who set the fires could find about the road. Several times motorists unaware of a dying bonfire that no longer emitted smoke had drove through them only for their vehicles to catch fire. A day after celebration of anger or happiness on the streets, the streets were littered with the ashes of burned tyres and tyre wires the fire could not reduce to ashes.

It was one of these fires that Yagu stumbled

on and fell into. The fire had waned, but was still strong enough to consume a man, especially a dying man like Yagu that could not struggle out of it. He died in the fire, his face turned up like a broken mirror in which Bivan's house may view itself.

Chapter Thirteen

The street Badaru took to avoid meeting the figure ahead of him was a narrow street with shading trees and houses that made it quite menacing particularly on a turbulent night like this. Apart from being narrow and dark, the street was full of potholes. It was an old tarred street that the tar had worn out completely in several places. The road in the daytime looked like potsherds that no patching – something common on the country's roads, could stitch. It had gotten to that stage of disrepair that it was better off with the remaining tar scrapped than with the fragmented pieces that donned it like a tortoise's back. Badaru's legs kept knocking against raised grounds that had resisted the wears and tears of rain and use, and sinking into troughs that rain and use had bored on the road.

Walking, or as perhaps fitted his progress, crawling through the street, Badaru had the haunting sense of walking through a tunnel or crawling out of a well he had been thrown into. If in addition to the fright of going through this narrow meandering street full of shadowy, menacing figures, he had known he would run into a band of youths dressed like soldiers, perhaps he would not have taken it. Christian youths dressed in military uniform had gone out to avenge the burning of their church by Moslem youths and to loot whatever they could find. They chose to dress in military instead of police uniform because there was little respect by the public for the police who were generally seen as excessively corrupt.

Badaru's obsession as he crept through the street was to be able to reach home with what he had stolen in the wedding reception arena. As he walked, he was thinking of Talgon and the close shave he had with death in the wedding reception arena. Though Talgon was his friend, he had always nursed a secret envy and resentment of him because of his popularity. His envy and resentment of Talgon tended to rise in tandem with latter's popularity. In the wedding arena, his envy turned murderous. When they got to the wedding arena, many people they met knew Talgon, but no one seemed to know him. While some people hailed his friend from where they were sitting or standing, others came and shook hands with him where they were. Badaru received only careless, cursory glances he was not even sure were meant for him or he just happened to be in the way of their object. If they were for him, he was not sure there was esteem for him in them.

In addition to his popularity, Talgon was not a Moslem. This was another cause for Badaru's secret resentment of his friend. As a Moslem, he had always been something of a fanatic and had several times preached to Talgon who said he believed in the religion of his ancestors to embrace

Islam, but Talgon had not yielded to his sermons and converted. Two days to this religious crisis, he had again preached to Talgon to convert to Islam, but was shocked by what Talgon said.

'Because of the fraud at their centre, I can never patronize these foreign religions you have so much faith in,' Talgon had said in a tone that sounded arrogant to him. 'I cherish honesty and wherever I smell dishonesty, I steer clear of that place. To have you believe in any of these religions, they terrorize you with hell when such a place does not exist. I wonder why these religions have not been charged with terrorism. The war on terror should have begun with them.'

'Well, you know the war on terror was declared by a certain Bush,' he had said in a voice that was a little strained. Bush knowing there is hell won't dare declare war on any of these religions that talk of hell. Any bush that declares the sort of war you talk of, fire from hell would light upon that bush and you know the delight of fire in a bush.'

Though he had not shown hostility to Talgon in his reply, he was shocked and grieved by what Talgon said and vowed vengeance. His opportunity for vengeance came when the wedding reception arena turned into a slaughter house. It was he that first hit Talgon on the nape of his neck as the latter was trying to help the old man that had been knocked down by the stampede in the reception arena and was about to be trampled to death. Since Talgon did not believe in hell, probably because he could not see it, he would send him there so that he would believe. He was aiming a fatal blow on Talgon's head when someone behind him hit him on his head and he fell down, losing consciousness.

Now moving on this treacherous street, he was happy he had not only survived the attack, but had gotten money that would make life better for him. When he takes the money to his house, he would take Talgon's eyeglasses to his wife if she was not consumed by the crisis. He would tell her how he nearly lost his own life while trying to save her husband's life, but all his efforts were in vain. Talgon's wife was such a woman he would not mind having. Now that he was a wealthy man, she would find it hard to resist him.

Towards the end of the street, someone who must have heard his approach stepped out of the shadows of the street and with a deep, booming voice ordered him to stop walking. His stomach turned and his heart begun to throb violently. The man snapped on a torch and poured its light on his face. Other people emerged from surrounding shadows and sidled up to the man with the torchlight.

'We are soldiers on patrol,' said the man with the torchlight. 'Identify yourself.'

Badaru was a little relieved to know he was

being stopped by soldiers on patrol and not by some hoodlums. There was nothing strange in soldiers on patrol hiding in the dark and springing surprise on a suspect. Security enforcement in the country in recent times had become a hide-and-seek game. He had seen police in Nakana hiding among flowers to spring surprises on offending motorists unaware of their presence. Even the Road Safety Brigade these days rarely position themselves in conspicuous places where they would be seen from a distance. Rather they would find a road bend that screened them from the view of approaching motorists so that it would be too late for a motorist who was not wearing his seatbelt to strap it across his chest. 'I am Badaru,' he said.

'Badaru, from where are you coming in a night like this?'

'From a wedding ceremony, 'said Badaru.

'Wedding ceremonies take place in the daytime; why is it that it is now you are going home?'

Before Badaru could answer the man with the torchlight, one of the fellows with him said, 'the funeral ceremony is over, but the drummer is still hanging around, does he want to marry the widow? Answer us Badaru.'

Badaru began to say something, but was interrupted by the man with the torchlight. 'If your name is Badaru, you must be a Moslem.'

If Badaru had known he was not before soldiers, but hoodlums, he would not have answered this question as readily as he did. Before a mob in a religious crisis, it was always a difficult question to answer if the person confronted by the mob did not know the character of the mob before him – whether the mobsters be Christians or Moslems. If he said he was a Christian and it was a Moslem mob, he would be killed. If he said he was a Moslem and he was before a Christian mob, he would be killed. So, he had to ascertain the character of the mob before venturing an answer. Even when he had properly determined the character of the mob and declared himself an adherent of its faith, he might nevertheless suffer ruination if the mob suspected he was lying and decided to test his claim. There was the story of a Moslem who when confronted by a Christian mob said he was a Christian. One of the mobsters doubting his claim decided to test it by reciting: *In the name of the Father, the Son and* .... The man was asked to complete the recitation and he said *the mother*.

Badaru believing he was before law enforcement agents said, without hesitation, that he was a Moslem. Immediately he said he was a Moslem, shouts of, 'Kill him! Kill the infidel' rang out of the hoodlums. Hidden machetes and cutlasses descended on Badaru reducing him to a heap of flesh and blood.

None of the religious fanatics expected Badaru to carry so much money with him. So, it did not occur to any to search him for money. It was by a fortuitous stray of the eyes that the fanatic with the torch saw the bulge in Badaru's pocket and decided to check to see what was bulging in the pocket. To his surprise he discovered Badaru's pocket was bursting with money. He tried hiding his discovery from the others, but one of the fanatics had seen what he saw. So, the money had to be shared among them.

Chapter Fourteen

Talgon having not been seen at home after the crisis, early in the morning the following day his family and Umaru his neighbor went out to look for him. It was one of those dull days in which the night seemed to be peeping into the day only to draw back. Bursts of light and shadows of darkness mingled in a friendship that was both warm and cold. Trees according as they were moved by the wind sang in a toast of life or mourned in a hiss of death.

Talgon's family and Umaru first went to the wedding ceremony ground to look for him, but all they saw there were patches of blood spotting the wedding reception arena like a leopard skin and enveloping it in an atmosphere of desolation and gloom. The dead bodies had been carried away to Bangora General Hospital's mortuary. Though death left the arena several hours ago, the footprints it left behind were very visible and frightful. The search team fled the gory scene and went to the mortuary, but most of the corpses they saw at the mortuary were either burned or mutilated beyond recognition. It was therefore impossible to know whether Talgon was among the corpses or not. Hoping he was not, they decided to go in search of him farther afield. They split themselves into two search-teams. One team was to go into the town and search the streets, uncompleted buildings and police stations while the other team was to search the bushes and river Bangora. It was like that every time there was a religious riot. People went about looking for missing relations in bushes, rivers, uncompleted buildings, the streets, mortuaries and police stations.

It was Talgon's first son Barnabas and Umaru Talgon's neighbor that went to look for him in the bushes and river Bangora. None of them had slept well the previous night Talgon having not returned from the wedding ceremony he attended. Despite the weariness of their bodies and the fear in their hearts, they were talking all the way from the mortuary to the countryside of Bangora. They were both shocked and revolted by what they saw at the mortuary.

'Religious riots in this country are like volcanic eruptions,' said Barnabas.

'What is a volcanic eruption?' asked Umaru.

'Volcanic eruption is the violent opening up of a mountain and pouring out of liquid fire from the womb of the earth which burned to death any living thing within its path or range.'

'From where did you get this strange knowledge?' Umaru asked, fascinated by what Barnabas had said.

'I am studying geology in the university and this is one of the things we are taught,' said Barnabas.

'Our children are surely learning strange things at school,' said Umaru, losing none of his fascination. 'Who would have thought a mountain is sitting over a lake of fire buried deep in the bowels of the earth?'

'Religion here is an active volcano,' said Barnabas. 'Often there is no telling when it would erupt. But what can always be foretold is that whenever it erupts, it will claim and maim many lives. A stream of smoke shoots into the air from the cone of religious sentiments and fanaticism. While the people are still looking in awe wondering what it is, there is a loud blast that sounds like the blast of thunder. But it is the blast of an erupting religious volcano. People begin to run helter-skelter. But for many, it is always too late. Glowing lava, fiery rivulets run down the mountain of religious fanaticism at ninety kilometers per hour roasting people, animals and trees on the path of the volcanic flow. A dense cloud of volcanic ash laden with gas swoops down the mountain slopes killing people by abrasion, impact and sheer heat. The most awesome sight to the few people who would survive the eruption to tell the story is the volcanic lightning. Out of the fiery volcanic ash and gas, volcanic lightning flares out like the tongue of a snake striking anything within reach. A man struck by volcanic lightning, all in flames would run about for a while screaming before falling to the ground where he is burned to ashes. The volcanic eruption might last for only a few hours but by the time it is over, the whole town would be covered with volcanic ash and debris. A pall of sadness like volcanic gas would hang over the town like the shadow of death for days after the eruption.'

'The school is giving our children knowledge we their parents can never hope to have,' said Umaru. 'Can you tell me more about this volcanic eruption to which you likened our recurrent religious conflicts?'

Barnabas in simple, clear terms explained to Umaru what a volcanic eruption is, how it takes place and the regions of the earth prone to it.

Although Umaru was genuinely grieved by Talgon's disappearance, as a Moslem who resented blasphemy, he did not see anything wrong with killing people for God's sake if indeed some infidels said some of the things they were alleged to have said against God and his messengers. 'It is wonderful to know that the earth carries such fire in its womb and that it can vomit it the way you are saying,' he said, excited by what Barnabas had told him. 'It only shows there is God and we must defend him from infidels working day and night for the devil. But God, who can plant fire inside the womb of the earth.'

'But if God is so powerful to plant fire in the bowels of the earth, he doesn't need our protection. It's we that need his protection.'

'I pray your father has not passed his madness to you,' said Umaru, taking on a severe look. 'I pray he is still alive so that he can have another opportunity to repent and be a good Moslem. The analogy of the volcanic eruption you just placed before me my son is very apt,' he continued speaking after a momentary pause. 'The earth and people living on earth have similar ways of expressing anger. Whether it is the earth speaking in anger or the people, it is God chastising mankind. The heart of man is dark and evil. There is the need for the light of God to shine on it; there is need for God to pour the fire in his mouth to consume our evil deeds. Since God cannot use the earth or mountains here to chastise us, he is using people to chastise us.'

'If God chastise us this way, how will the devil chastise us?'

'Your father has a good heart; follow his heart. But he has a bad mind; don't follow his mind because it will only take you to hell,' said Umaru with passion Barnabas found frightening. 'We are like little children. For our own good we need this chastisement now and then.'

'Whenever men go to war to defend God from men who want to destroy him, the picture that comes to my mind is that of a cat owner going to war with a rat he is complaining is chasing his cat to kill it,' said Barnabas. 'I find it difficult to understand how men can protect God from fellow men God created; men whose lives are said to be in God's custody.'

'What did you say you are reading in the university?'

'Geology.'

'Well, it's either what you are reading is bad for you or what your father has being telling you is bad for you. If we find him alive, I must tell him to stop corrupting you. If his soul is beyond recovery from hell, he shouldn't send yours there as well. No one will wish his own child to inherit him in hell.'

By now they were near the bridge over river Bangora. They split into two. Umaru began tracing the river downstream on the bank they approached the river while Barnabas trekked to the other end of the bridge and began tracing the river downstream like Umaru. The riversides stretching to houses well off the river were under cultivation all year round. Carrots, sugarcane, onions, tomatoes and assorted vegetables were all grown on the fertile alluvial soils of the river according to the season proper for their growth. In the dry season, almost all the vegetables needed in Bangora were grown along this river irrigated with water from the river. It was said the river was the major incentive that made the first settlers of Bangora to settle where the town now was.

On a normal day, the riversides like a beach full of tourists, would have been bustling with farmers in their farms and women who had come to buy one farm produce or the other. But today the riversides were deserted by farmers and women who had either been killed or maimed by the religious conflagration or were at home mourning a relation that had been killed or nursing their own injuries or those of relations or in the hospital attending to maimed relations or being attended to by relations.

Walking on the banks of the river, Barnabas and Umaru were walking through people's farms of tomatoes, onions, carrots and sugarcane. The boundary of each farm was well marked off by its owner to avoid encroachment by a neighbor. There were so many farms it was a wonder to Barnabas that each farm owner knew his farm. It was like everyone in Bangora owned a parcel of land along the river. As they walked, they looked into furrows and peered into thick stocks of sugarcane searching for Talgon. Occasionally they looked into the river. It was not long the rains were gone and so there was still water in the river. A little far off from the bridge, the body of a man was seen by Umaru lying close to the river bank half-covered with water, half-eaten by the knives that killed him. Even from the river bank, neither the colour nor the size of the corpse in the river generated fear in Umaru that the corpse might be that of his neighbor. 'Barnabas, look at that corpse in the river,' he called out to Barnabas who was peering into a thick stock of sugarcane.

Barnabas looked and saw the body in the river and immediately knew it was not his father's. He quickly looked away. The corpse was as revolting to sight as the revolt that claimed its owner. He had his own thoughts about God and religion which he would not dare express even to his father who was seen by people like Umaru as a pagan. Moments like this stoke the fire of such thoughts. Now flames of such thoughts were flaring in his mind. It was difficult to say whether God, if there is such a being, has brought peace to the world or was only fanning the embers of hatred. All the flashpoints of the earth were either where God was a native or where there was a fanatical attachment to him. The man lying inside the river was killed in the gruesome manner he was by people who believed in God. If God's followers killed in this way, what was to be expected from those that did not believe in God and therefore were called children of the devil by those who believed in God? The wind like an embittered mistress whined round him in a manner that further distressed him. Like him, the wind today was restless. Earlier in the day the harmattan wind was restful, lying about with the marked comfort of a monarch without a care. Occasionally it stirred as if to remind itself it was still alive before slumping again to its delightful state of rest. But now the raw harmattan wind was up, swirling around people like bees with a sort of resentment that was sensible.

Further downstream, Barnabas and Umaru heard the cry of a woman and a child in pains inside a big hole that was probably dug many years ago by bricklayers when the riverside was yet to be completely taken over by farmers. It was on

Barnabas's side of the river. So Umaru crossed the river to join Barnabas at the mouth of the hole where the woman and her little child were. Several times the woman with her child clutching to her would place her hand on the wall of the hole and raised herself up in an effort to claw her way out of the hole, but she would cry out in pain and fall back to the floor of the pit. It was clear this was where she and the child slept the previous night. They were both covered with dust and looked woebegone. In the course of the night, the woman must have attempted several times to crawl out of the pit with her child, but failing to do so each time and falling back to the bottom of the pit as she had done now – hence their dusty appearance. It looked like she had a fracture or a dislocation in one of her legs which had prevented her from crawling out of the hole.

Barnabas entered the hole to help the woman and her child out. Umaru remained at the mouth of the hole where he took hold of the woman's raised hands and pulled her and the child out of the hole when Barnabas hoisted them up. Out of the hole, the woman could not stand on her feet.

'What happened?' asked Umaru.

`Some men chanting *Allahu akbar* chased me and my child when I was returning from the market into this pit. I fell into the pit and they raped me, chanting *Allahu akbar*. After they had finished with me, they left me and my child to die in this hole.'

'God is great,' murmured Umaru.

'So, it is the greatness of God that pushed this poor woman and her little child into this pit?' said Barnabas. 'It is the greatness of God that wrought this outrage on this poor woman and her child.'

'These men if they are Moslems have done a great wrong. In war, Islam forbids attack on women and children.'

'The problem with us is that we are nihilists,' said Barnabas. 'But we put on the garb of being religious while we go on to behave according to our unbelieving nature. God owns our lips, but the devil owns our hearts.'

'Where do you live?' asked Umaru.

'I live at Unguwar Wake.'

'How do we get her home to be attended to?' asked Umaru.

'I think the best thing is to get her to the road and get a bus for her,' said Barnabas.

'That is if we can find one,' said Umaru.

'That is another problem,' said Barnabas. 'The violence of yesterday is keeping everyone off the road. A taxi would have been the best vehicle to carry them,' he continued after a brief pause. 'But even without this crisis, there are no more taxis in this town. Yet, ten years ago taxis were everywhere in this town. All the indices point to the fact that as a country the commonwealth is rolling back, shrinking like the water of this river with the coming of the dry season. Without water in this river, life is bound to be hell for all the living creatures of the river. Our roads are full of cars, but there is no car to board because the cars on the road are private cars. There is a long train of cars on the road which is almost empty because every coach of that train carries only a passenger.'

'It is sad.'

'It is indeed sad.'

'What are we to do then?'

'We have to get them to the road. Who knows? A vehicle may turn up.'

Together Barnabas and Umaru began lugging the woman and her child to the road.

'Thank you very much,' said the woman as she was helped to the road.

'It is our pleasure,' said Barnabas.

'I am sorry to be such a burden to you.'

'You need help. We have to help you.'

'What were you looking for when you found me and my child?'

'We are looking for my father.'

'And now I have taken you from that search. Wretched me. Please, leave me and go look for him. He might be in need of help than me.'

Both Barnabas and Umaru could see the woman meant what she was saying. There was care in her voice and worry on her face.

Such a good-hearted woman thought Barnabas. And some ruffians were so heartless to put her in this condition. 'We can't do such as you requested,' he said firmly. 'We must get you to the road and on a vehicle before we continue our search for him. By the way, do you have any money with you?'

The woman shook her head. 'They took my money after raping me.'

Barnabas was seized by a murderous rage. After looting her little property, they looted her purse, perhaps also chanting *Allahu akbar*. 'We may be believers in God, but there is no doubt that we are pagans of honesty,' he murmured under his breath. 'Don't worry, we will pay your fare home,' he said in an emotive voice. He had 200 hundred baduns with him. A bus fare from the bridge to Unguwar Wake would not be more than forty baduns.

'Thank you very much,' said the woman.

'It is our pleasure to be of help,' said Barnabas.

On the road, there was no vehicle in sight. After waiting by the roadside for more than thirty minutes, it was an ambulance carrying people injured during the crisis to the hospital that carried the woman and her child.

Chapter Fifteen

One of the places Talgon's wife and children inside the town went to look for him was the police station. After a riot such as that of the previous day, the police would arrest several people thought to have precipitated or participated in the crisis. Most of the people arrested were those found on the streets during and shortly after the crisis. Talgon was not in his house when the crisis erupted. So he might have been arrested by the police if he was found on the street.

When they got to the police station, the first thing they saw on the counter were Talgon's eyeglasses lying close to a police baton also on the counter. Talgon's wife heart leapt with joy. Her husband was still alive. The police may be a lot of trouble, but what was that compared to her husband's death? Feeling light headed, she asked a woman sergeant at the counter about the owner of the eyeglasses.

'The woman sergeant well into her forties was still a spinster. She was a pretty woman who had her opportunities of getting married to one of the numerous men that toasted her during her prime, but frittered away all those opportunities thinking time was yet plenty for tying the nuptial knots. When she found out she had ran out of time, desperation cheapened her before men who would have taken her more seriously. In her village, old women sang this song of her to their daughters:

> She was a blooming flower
> Bearing the sweet scents of youth
> Bees from far and near
> Like flocks of hungry vultures
> Swarmed over her flowering bud
> She failed to trap a poaching bee
> Now she is a withering flower
> And all the bees are gone.

When the woman sergeant lost all hope of landing a man to marry, she became cynical and cruel in her attitude towards people. Benjamin, the last man who she hoped to marry but who like others turned her down died in mysterious circumstances. Benjamin had met her when he was still a student in the university. He had promised to marry her after his university education. Since then she had stalked him the way a hunter would stalk a prized game. But Benjamin was not to be the trophy she pined for. The moment he graduated from the university, he turned his back on her. Her friends told her that Benjamin has been saying behind her back that she was a worn-out *pantie* and he would not buy stale tomatoes when there were so many fresh tomatoes in the market. In fact, that he would not board a rickety taxi to the market when there were limousines plying the road for the same fares. Suddenly Benjamin became sick.

There were rumors s she had a hand in his sickness. As if to confirm the rumors, she went to the hospital where he was bedridden and asked him if he would change his mind and marry her. Unable to speak, Benjamin shook his head. She told him on his sickbed that he was now on board the limousine that would take him to a bigger market in the hereafter where there were garden-fresh tomatoes to be purchased. Benjamin died the following day and the woman sergeant began an internecine war against anyone unfortunate to be involved with her. Now looking at Talgon's wife, she affected the air of an old witch to whom death was humor. 'You mean the owner of these glasses?' she asked Talgon's wife with scorn on her face.

'Yes,' said Talgon's wife.

'He is dead,' she said with feelings near happiness in her heart.

'What!' cried Talgon's wife. Her children with her began to cry also.

'Please, can you help me by going to cry outside?' said the woman sergeant, rubbing her two palms in a pleading gesture that in the circumstance was provocative. 'Our ears are already full of lamentations we didn't cause.'

'But we have been to the mortuary,' said Talgon's wife, ignoring the provocative plea of the woman sergeant. 'We did not see his corpse at the mortuary and that's why we are here.'

'Maybe you didn't look well,' said the woman sergeant. 'You know the eyes see only what the mind wants them to see. Since your mind would not let your eyes see his corpse, I will ask the police constable who took his corpse to the mortuary to accompany you to the mortuary again and show you his corpse. That way we will be free of the noise I am sure you would want to torture us with. Sani!' she bellowed; 'come and take them to the mortuary.'

A walloping police constable came out of an adjacent office to the counter where Talgon's wife and children were with the woman sergeant. He was out of all size with his lack of rank in the police force. Talgon's daughter who had come to associate size with rank in the police force was taken aback seeing this ogre of a man without a pip on his uniform.

'Take them to the mortuary and show them the corpse of the man that owned these glasses,' the woman sergeant said, waving her hand at Talgon's family and handing Talgon's eyeglasses to the constable.

'*Oyah*,' said the constable, waving a march-out order at Talgon's family that was as inappropriate for the task he was asked to perform as a kick was to an already opened door. But since he was a man always under the command of others with no one to command, he might be excused for giving command to hapless people he had been commanded to take to the mortuary.

The constable marched them out of the police station as if they were criminals he was taking to the gallows. He was whistling and belching in the most disagreeable manner as he herded Talgon's family along the road to the mortuary. When he stopped whistling, he was snorting as if the air on the road was not enough for him. A bird flew past them chirping noisily as if it were pursued by an unseen predator. The constable cursed it as if it were responsible for his general uninspiring condition.

Near the hospital, Talgon's daughter saw someone like her father taking a side street going in the direction of their house. 'Mummy!' she called her mother, nudging her with her fingers at the same time; 'see daddy over there,' she pointed at the person who was walking with his head bent low.

Talgon's wife looked in the direction her daughter was pointing and saw the figure her daughter was pointing at. No doubt the man looked like her husband and was wearing the type of clothes he wore the previous day; but already convinced by the police that he was dead, the only thought that came into her mind was that it was not him she was seeing but his ghost.

But it was Talgon hurrying home. He knew his family or whatever remains of it would be very anxious having not seen him since the crisis. He wanted to leave Beckin very early in the morning and go home, but she had insisted on treating his wound and bandaging it. After treating and bandaging the wound with impressive expertise, she still full of paranoia over the possible appearance of her husband after he had left, would not allow him to go. He had to take her round the house to convince her that her husband who she believed was a malignant spirit hovering over her was not anywhere near the house before she could gain some measure of courage. After that, by pleasant manners and tales of her miserable life with her husband, she had kept him in the house until he discovered the morning was far gone. When he was leaving, she had insisted he leaves the child in her house because she was not sure he would return if he left with the child.

'It is not your father,' her mother wept. 'It is his ghost. You heard what the police said and we are here with his eyeglasses.'

'Have you seen his corpse?' asked the daughter.

The constable looked at her sharply. 'Are you saying we are liars?' he asked the girl with what looked like shock and anger on his face. 'The only thing that western education has brought is unbelief. Whatever it is worth, the unbelief it is planting in our children has made it worthless.'

'I have not seen his corpse,' said her mother in a voice full of grief. 'But the police said it is in the mortuary and that's why they are taking us there. Besides, what would your father's eyeglasses be doing beside a corpse that is not his?'

But her daughter was no longer with them. She had broken into a run after Talgon. She called him as she ran towards him. The police constable, Talgon's wife and son believing the figure to be a ghost stood looking, expecting the figure they were still seeing to dissolve into thin air, but it did not. Instead, Talgon on hearing the voice of his daughter turned and called her.

'Well, well; this is something,' said the constable. 'So it was not his corpse the eyeglasses were lying by?'

'It appears it was not,' said Talgon's wife, excitedly. She was hopping about on one spot. One time her hands were on her head; the other time they were flailing about her excitedly. Talgon and his daughter were moving towards them from the other side of the road.

'And you are sure the eyeglasses are his?' she heard the constable asking.

A red light sprung up in her head. What is the constable getting at? she wondered. 'I am not sure they are his glasses,' she said, cautiously.

'But you were so sure a while ago.'

Talgon's wife did not say anything.

'Well, he is coming. He will tell us whether they are his eyeglasses or not. Not that whatever he says would make much difference.'

Talgon's wife knowing her husband would still claim the eyeglasses as his even if she were to tell him the danger of doing so did not look for an opportunity to tell him to disown the eyeglasses.

Soon Talgon and his daughter were with his wife and the constable. Talgon's wife rushed to her husband. 'What happened? We thought you were dead. We were even going to the mortuary to identify your corpse among the many corpses there when Menwa saw you.'

'I am not dead,' said Talgon. 'But yesterday I went through a harrowing experience I had never gone through in my life and may never go through. I saw death, but it asked me to go.'

'Thanks be to God,' said Talgon's wife. 'What happened to your leg?'

'Enough of the excitements,' said the constable, stepping up to Talgon. 'I trust these are your eyeglasses?' he asked, holding Talgon's eyeglasses before him.

'Yes, they are my glasses,' said Talgon, delighted to see his eyeglasses.

'You are under arrest,' said the constable, flashing his teeth in what was neither a grin nor a cry of pain.

'What for?' asked Talgon a look of alarm taking over his face.

'These eyeglasses were found by the body of a man who was hacked to death. Initially we thought the eyeglasses belonged to the man that was hacked to death. So when your wife and children turned up at our station claiming the eyeglasses are yours, we assumed you were the man that was hacked to death. But now that you are still alive and like your wife and children, you are claiming the eyeglasses are yours, you must have killed the man beside whose body we found the eyeglasses.'

'This is terrible,' said Talgon. 'Why would I do a thing like that?'

'Why should your eyeglasses be found by his

body if you would not do a thing like that? By the way, it would interest you to know the man's pockets were found turned inside out. We suspect he was killed for his money. Anyone in Bivan's house can kill for money and that includes you.'

'But if I killed him for his money, I would have the money on me. Right now, the only money on me is less than a hundred baduns and you don't suppose I will kill a human being for that kind of money,' said Talgon pulling his pockets out and showing the constable the money he had.

'You could have hidden the money you stole from the dead man somewhere.'

'Well, I did not hide any money anywhere,' said Talgon. 'Why should I when I have a house I can take it? As you can see, I have not been home and that's why my family is out looking for me.'

The constable was getting irritated by the unruffled manner Talgon was speaking to him. This guy needs to be softened to realize the kind of trouble he is in, he thought. But he could not do the softening here. All he could do now was to issue veiled threats. The man's family would lynch him if he attempted anything here. 'When we get to the station, you will appreciate better how it's possible to hide the money somewhere,' he said, squeezing his face into an ugly scowl. 'You will appreciate how it's possible you might be walking with the money in your pants now.'

Talgon's daughter was now regretting running after her father and bringing him to this new trouble. If she had not ran after him, he would not be in this trouble.

'*Oyah*, let's go to the station,' said the constable, cutting Talgon off from his family and herding him in the direction of the police station.

'You can't take him away,' cried Talgon's wife. 'He has killed no one.'

'The eyeglasses he left by his victim is our proof,' said the constable, taking hold of Talgon's hand though he had not given him any sign he would run away.

'I will be fine,' said Talgon to his wife. 'You go home and take care of the children. Later you can come and see me at the police station.'

But Talgon's wife and children would not leave him and go home. A policeman of Bivan's house was not to be trusted, thought the wife. If the policeman believed her husband had the money on his body as he seemed to, he would kill him on the way to the police station to make away with the money he believed he had with him. 'We will go to the station with you,' she said. 'How do we tell anyone we saw you and you were taken to the police station on a charge of murder and we proceeded home?'

'Isn't it proper we finish our trip to the mortuary and see the corpse by which the eyeglasses were found?' asked Talgon's son who had spoken little since they left the police station to the mortuary.

It seems what he said shocked the constable, for a startled expression jumped into his face. But what the boy said made sense to him and he agreed that they go to the hospital beside whose fence they were standing.

At the hospital, the corpse of Badaru was brought out. Though he had been badly mutilated, Talgon recognized him almost immediately. 'But,this is Badaru!' he cried.

'Badaru?' whined his wife in shock. When she first came to check for her husband among the corpses, she was shown this same corpse, but she did not recognize it as Badaru's. Nasty as she was, there was some truth in what the woman sergeant said about the eyes seeing only what the mind wants them to see.

The constable looked at them not knowing what to make of the drama unfolding before him.

Chapter Sixteen

Barnabas and Umaru did not wait long on the road before they got a motorcycle to carry the distressed woman and her child home. After she was taken away, they went back to continue their search.

Somehow Barnabas was not unduly worried about his father. The calmness in his heart told him his father was still alive. From experience, whenever he lost a thing and became unduly worried, he would never find that thing again. It was as if by intuition it had been communicated to him the thing would not be found, hence his excessive worry. But if he lost a thing and was less worried, he would almost certainly find what was lost. It was as if by intuition it had been communicated to him the thing would be found, hence his lack of worry. If his father was dead, he won't be feeling the way he was.

As he searched for his father after they returned from helping the woman and her child to the road, Barnabas kept wondering where he had seen the woman they helped before. The moment he saw her in the hole, he had a vague feeling of seeing her before now, but thought he was merely suffering from a sense of *dejavu*. But now with the woman gone, he was almost certain he had seen her before only he could not say where and under what circumstances. Poor woman he thought. She would never be able to live over this harrowing experience as long as she lives.

What was the problem with Bivan's house? he kept asking himself. Why do we profess with our lips that we love God only to tell him with our behavior that we don't know him; that he does not exist? Why do we profess to follow spirits only to set our dogs on them? Those who have education do not think better than those who don't. The previous year, Boyama the primehead of Bivan's house wanted to amend the country's constitution to give him power to appoint and remove the Chief Justice of the country without reference to the house of archery and the national labor union had gone on strike over this. The leader of the national association of Bivan's house students without the arithmetic of simple English had gone on air saying, 'more powers for Boyama or no more powers for Boyama, everyone should quiet down.' The central government could go ahead and amend the constitution.

'The leader of an association of hunters would not issue such a statement,' he murmured. Students were fire-eating bigots that were as easily roused into a religious mayhem as a tribe of baboons answering calls that a strayed member of the tribe has been killed. This crisis that started from his university over a religious argument was typical of the rabid religious sensibilities of Bivan's house university campuses. In Hamze University, students barely had light three hours of the day. The toilets were stinking because there was no water to flush them. About eight students shared a room meant for only two students. More than five hundred students were crammed into lecture theatres meant for only two hundred students. No student had ever rioted over any of these poor amenities and conditions of living. But upon an argument over who is the true messiah of the world between Jesus Christ and Mohammed – foreign prophets the students shared no common ancestry with, there was a riot that claimed many lives. Meanwhile in the countries where these prophets came from, no student was rioting over them. It was so sad and embarrassing. It was so disturbing to think of. His philosophy teacher once said members of Bivan's house were imitations of human beings. He was now beginning to see the truth of that assertion. A university which is a factory of ideas in other parts of the world was a nursery of idiocy and imbecile behavior in Bivan's house. Instead of being citadels of learning, Bivan's house's universities were incubators of ignorance and facile thoughts. Elsewhere a university as a tertiary institution is a place for tertiary minds. But here it was a place for primary minds. 'Well, being so badly off on earth, perhaps the final salvation of Bivan's house may be in the next world,' he muttered, bitterly. 'Perhaps, that is why we should hold so tight to God. But are we? Which God sanctions this sort of cruel attack on a woman and her child?' he murmured in deep thought.

Barnabas was so gripped by these thoughts

that he was no longer walking but standing on one spot, his mind intense and probing. Umaru observing he had moved ahead of him looked back to see what had kept him behind. He was surprised to see him standing on one spot, his eyes fixed on the ground.

'What's the matter?' he called.

'Oh, nothing,' said Barnabas, a little startled. He shook his head and continued the search.

'I don't think your father would be found in these parts,' said Umaru, after they had moved further down the river. 'As you can see, we have gone beyond the stretch of the town in our search without finding him. Perhaps, we should go back into the town and see whether your mother and siblings had fared better in their search.'

'I think you are right,' said Barnabas. 'From what we have seen so far, it seems the violence of yesterday did not reach the river the way we thought it did.'

With Umaru leading the way, they both turned and began walking towards the town.

On the way, Barnabas kept raking his brains to remember where he knew the woman that was raped. He was almost giving up when he remembered. It was at a makeshift restaurant he had gone to have a meal. She was the proprietor of the restaurant. She was very courteous to him and every customer that came to eat in her restaurant. To whoever she gave food, she dropped a curtsy. Her manners stood her as a woman who was well brought up and one who knew how to attend to the pleasures of her customers. Now recalling who the woman was, Barnabas' anger over what happened to her boiled over. He was now panting with hate. With a lot of violence in his voice and countenance, he started swearing and cursing those who violated and robbed her.

'What's the matter?' Umaru asked, taken aback by Barnabas' outburst.

'I know the woman we helped out of the hole a while ago.'

'Where do you know her?'

'In her restaurant. She sells food in a restaurant I once went to eat. She is such a nice woman.'

'I see,' said Umaru. 'I sometimes wonder why good people are often the victims of bad people. Well, such is life. The sheep is often eaten by the hyena.'

'But why should life be so?'

'I don't know. All I know is that injustice is an integral part of life as much as poison is an integral part of the snake or odor an integral part of the skunk. To even become great in terms of having a big name, you must suffer one form of injustice or the other. To be very rich, you must take what belongs to others. On earth, often it is the righteous that find themselves in the pits of hell and sinners in the bosoms of heaven.'

'You are right about injustice being an integral part of life. Someone said even to be born is an act of injustice to the person given birth to. But even with this knowledge, one is always tormented why life has to be this way.'

Not far from the bridge, they met a man who was nearly roasted to death by fire. Immediately Barnabas saw him, he reminded him of a youngster who two years ago caught fire while sitting on the roof of a moving campaign bus. One of the big feast candidates of Mokoma state for that year election had hired long buses for his campaign. Wherever the buses were moving, layabouts, political supporters of the candidate and excitement-seeking political thugs got on top of the buses for a sort of merry-go-round political jamboree. It was on one of these political jamborees on top of the buses that the buses came by a low-flying electric wire that set the youngster standing on top of one of the buses ablaze. Screaming and shedding his clothes that were on fire, he escaped death by the skin of his teeth. But the whole of his skin came off with his clothes.

Unlike the youngster on the bus, the skin of the man on the road was not completely peeled off, but peeled according to the severity of the burns he suffered on different parts of his body. Where the burns were severe, the skin was peeled. Where they were not so severe, the skin was still there. This made him to be spotted red and black like a leopard and that was what was fearful about him. Those the uprising killed took the horror of the carnage with them to the great beyond. This man did not die, but walked the streets like a bad dream frightening whoever came across him.

Barnabas averted his eyes to avoid looking at the naked horror the man had been reduced to. The raw harmattan wind battering his ears moaned like a tortured swine, but its grating sound was far more pleasant than the fright that just walked past him.

Chapter Seventeen

At the mortuary Talgon was looking at the hideously mutilated corpse of Badaru in shock and perplexity. He had thought his friend was killed by the religious fanatics that attacked them at the wedding ground, but now it was clear he was mistaken. The corpse he saw at the wedding reception venue which he thought was Badaru's was burned; the corpse before him at the mortuary wasn't and it was Badaru's. It was either that Badaru was able to get away from the wedding reception venue during the melee of the attack, or like him was injured, but was later able to walk away from the reception venue. That his eyeglasses were found by the corpse of Badaru made it more likely that Badaru could not have gotten away during the wild stampede that followed the attack, for his eyeglasses only fell off his face when he was hit on the nape of his neck. So Badaru must have been wounded one way or the other and only later was able to leave the wedding reception venue. It was when he was leaving the venue that he must have seen his eyeglasses and carried them believing he was either dead or had escaped the attack and fled home.

'Oh, my friend,' wept Talgon. 'Who did this to you?'

'Who are you trying to take in by these tricks?'

asked the constable, unimpressed by Talgon's grief. 'We all know the trick of hiding meat in the mouth while looking for it in the plate. You know the monkey and his business: after ravaging the man's banana plantation, the monkey was found beside the ravaged plantation weeping for the owner of the plantation.'

'Believe me; he was my friend,' cried Talgon.

'I am not saying he was not your friend,' said the constable. 'Rather what I am saying is that children kill their parents and parents kill their children for money these days. We all know about ritual killings for money that are now rampant in the country.'

'Well, I did not kill him,' said Talgon. 'Besides, he had no money I could kill him for.'

'So you could kill for money?'

'I am only trying to tell you even if I am the sort of person that can kill for money, my friend had no money I could kill him for.'

'That's what you are saying. But your friend's pockets that are turned inside out are telling us a different story. But why am I wasting my time here talking to you when the station is a better place I will get the answers I want for my questions. *Oyah*, on our way,' said the constable crowding Talgon away from the mutilated body of Badaru to herd him out of the mortuary and the hospital to the police station.

Talgon, his eyes still on the mutilated corpse

of Badaru followed the constable grieving quietly for his friend. His family followed him.

At the police station, Talgon was to be taken to the Divisional Police Officer (DPO) who looking through the window of his office had seen the constable and Talgon coming towards the police station. Immediately he saw Talgon, he recognized him. They were in the army together before he left the army and joined the police force. His promotion in the police force was so rapid that within the span of twelve years he had risen from corporal to superintendent of police. As soon as he joined the force, he found that more than in the army, promotion in the police force was not based on hard work or competence, but the godfather one had among the top echelon of the force and how frequently one made returns to his godfathers. Because of returns he was making to his godfather, as a sergeant he was posted to a police command secondary school as the storekeeper. As the storekeeper, he dealt with the contractors that supplied food to the school and controlled what came in and went out of the store. Within a short time, he was able to put up a sprawling edifice in his village and was able to make good returns to his godfather that influenced his posting to the school. Doing so well by his godfather, his promotion was running so fast that by the time he became Assistant Superintendent of police, some of his mates were still sergeants. When he was promoted Deputy Superintendent of Police, he was posted out of the school on the ground that his new rank was higher than the position he was occupying. He was not happy. It appeared to him that somehow his godfather had the archaic idea that since he was so diligent in making returns, he should be promoted. But he was not making returns to be promoted, but to be allowed to remain a storekeeper in the school. As far as he was concerned, he preferred to remain an Assistant Superintendent of police if he had the assurance he would be allowed to remain the storekeeper of the school. There being no such assurance, he had accepted the promotion and gone to his new posting which was more like a death sentence. Though wearing a higher rank, he was now financially worse off than he was when wearing a lower rank. He could only compare his ironic situation to the frequent declaration by Bivan's house motor mechanics to vehicle owners seeking repairs of their vehicles that a used-motor spare part was better than a new one. In fact, his own mechanic had told him so when he wanted to change the steering shaft of his car. He had answered that since an old shaft was better than a new one, he might as well continue using his old shaft; for there was no sense dropping one old shaft for another. As the case was with motor spare parts, it was with the nation's leaders. An old leader in Bivan's house was always better than a new one. It was a country where new things decayed while old things flowered with youth.

There were talks in the police force that godfathers occasionally got godsons out of lucrative positions they had put them to nip any arrogance wealth might breed in the godson and to impress upon the godson that he could not do without the godfathers. In his own case, such a shrewd manoeuvre by a godfather was a deft move that must serve the godfather well. As an Assistant Superintendent of police in charge of the store, Superintendents and even Chief Superintendents of Police were running errands for him and answering *sir* when he called them. When life was proving intolerable in the new office he was posted, he went on his knees before his godfather that he be given a better posting. It was his genuflections before his godfather that earned him the posting to Bangora as DPO which, compared to his earlier posting, was something like being made the custodian of *Aladin* cave. It was not more than three weeks that he was posted to Bangora as DPO when he saw Talgon who he did not know live in Bangora being marched to the police station by the constable.

The moment he saw Talgon being brought to the station by the constable in a disagreeable manner, he called the Divisional Crime Officer (DCO) to his office and detailed him to handle the case of the man Constable Sani was bringing to the station and not refer it to him. But whatever he squeezed from the man, he must make returns to him because he also must make returns to superior officers at Police Headquarters.

'Yes, sir,' the DCO saluted the DPO and walked out of the office to execute the order. On

the corridor leading to the DPO's office, he met
Talgon and the constable taking him to the DPO.
Talgon's wife and children were not allowed into
the station, but left at the counter.

'Morning sir!' the constable saluted the DCO.

The DCO made a vague gesture that to the
constable was an acknowledgement of his salute.

'Who is he?' asked the DCO, pointing at
Talgon. Ordinarily, it would have been an
unnecessary question. As the DCO, if the man with
the constable was a suspect, the constable having
brought him to the station would first take him to
the DCO. If he was not a suspect, it was none of
his business who he was. But the new DPO on
reporting at the station gave standing instructions
that every matter coming to the station must be
reported to him directly and it was his prerogative
to assign the matter to the DCO or any other police
officer to handle. To ensure compliance with this
instruction, he had his boys in the station spying on
the DCO and other key officers of the station.
They were to report to him any finding of non-
compliance with his instructions they made from
their espionage. So far, he was yet to receive any
untoward report on the DCO who knew he was
being spied on. He also had asked his own boys to
spy on the DPO so that in the event of any
showdown, he would have a weapon to hit back at
the DPO.

The constable like every policeman at the

station knew of the directive by the DPO and that was why he was taking Talgon to the DPO direct. So when the DCO asked him who Talgon was, he told him he was a suspect he was taking to the DPO.

'The DPO is very busy right now and has detailed me to receive in-coming complaints,' said the DCO. 'So bring him to my office.'

The DCO was from the minority tribe of Welle while the constable was from the majority tribe of Kunsu. The constable usually driven by a superiority complex of being Kunsu which had ruled Bivan's house most of its history never thought much of contravening an officer that was not from the Kunsu tribe. In addition to the complex and airs of the constable, he did not know the counter instruction the DPO had just given the DCO. So, he said, 'What you are saying is contrary to the DPO's instructions that fresh suspects must be brought to him first. Sorry sir, I can't do what you said.'

The DCO though looking humble on the surface was inside an arrogant man who was sharply conscious of who he was. He would tell anyone that he had risen to his position in the police force by din of hard work and merit, not by bonanza and patronage. Anyone foolhardy enough to bite him would find his teeth tearing into the bitter pulp of his arrogance. The constable knew this, but obsessed by the superiority complex of his tribe had been driven to say what he said to the DCO.

'What you have just said shows you are a fool who ought not to have been recruited into the force. But imbeciles that came into the force by the corruption of our system, any intelligent policeman or woman knows he or she must obey the last command. Move with that man past me and you can consider yourself out of the force.'

The constable's heart was now beating very fast. What he had said to the DCO was very disrespectful and unbecoming. He knew very well that if a police commissioner asked a police inspector to take out some men on patrol to a particular location and a police superintendent later counter this instruction by commanding the inspector to take them to another location, the inspector must obey the command of the superintendent and not that of the commissioner. If the commissioner wants to know why he had disobeyed him, he would simply refer to the counter instruction of the superintendent who would now have to explain to the commissioner why he did what he did.

'I am very sorry sir,' said the constable, saluting the DCO and steering Talgon who had been watching the unfolding drama with interest towards the DCO's office.

Chapter Eighteen

Barnabas and Umaru thinking Talgon might have been found or he might have himself returned home, decided to go to the house first to know the current situation of things. When they did not find anybody at home, they knew he had not yet been found. They decided to go to the different places they earlier agreed the other search team should go. They went to about three places before they went to the police station where they found Talgon's wife and other children. Talgon's wife and daughter tired of standing were sitting on a bench in front of the station. The second son was still standing by the counter.

The moment Barnabas saw his mother sitting in front of the station, he knew their search at the station had turned up something. There was a visible improvement in his mien.

'Has he been found?' asked Barnabas from afar.

'Yes,' said the mother. 'But there's a big problem.'

'What's the problem?' asked Barnabas and Umaru together.

'His eyeglasses were found by Badaru's corpse and the police had arrested him for Badaru's murder.'

'Who is Badaru?' asked Barnabas.

'You may not know him. But he was a friend

of your father.'

'So Badaru was also killed,' murmured Umaru. 'Ah...'

'How did father's eyeglasses leave him and were found near the dead body of another man?' asked Barnabas.

'That's the mystery we are yet to unravel.'

'Who found the dead body and the eyeglasses beside it?'

'The police said they did and in truth it seemed they did.' She told her son and Umaru how she and her other children first saw the eyeglasses at the police station and identified them as Talgon's only for this act of theirs to lead to Talgon's arrest. While she was still talking, her son at the counter came out to join them outside. 'Have they brought him out to the counter since they took him inside?' she asked.

Her son shook his head.

'Well, we will continue to wait here until they bring him out,' said the mother.

'I think mummy it would be better for you to go home and prepare food for him,' said Barnabas. 'I believe he has not eaten today and from the nature of the allegation, we cannot hope to get him out of this station today. You go home and we will wait and see what we can do.'

What her son said made sense to Talgon's wife. She looked at her other children and Umaru and everyone seemed to agree with Barnabas.

She stood up and began walking towards the major road opposite the police station. After she left, it occurred to Barnabas that instead of sitting and waiting for Talgon to be brought out of the station, it was wise they look for a lawyer to handle the matter. The lawyers know what the police know about the law and therefore would be able to talk the law with them and get his father out. He communicated his thoughts to Umaru who shook his head.

'I have also thought of a lawyer,' said Umaru. 'But I have heard that there is nothing the police resent like a lawyer being brought into a matter when it is still this fresh and hot. It is like calling wolves when hyenas had just felled an antelope. The moment you bring in a lawyer, the police think you are not only trying to deny them any money they would extort from the suspect, but out to fight them and they would become unnecessarily difficult.'

'Even without a lawyer, they are difficult.'

'With him they would be more difficult.'

'If they are difficult with a lawyer, he would be more adept at handling them than we are.'

'But it cost a lot of money to engage a lawyer.'

'That's true. But I have a lawyer friend. I know he would assist me with any little money I can find.'

'You can go and call him then,' said Umaru. 'There's nothing like knowing people that matter when one is in trouble.'

Barnabas left for the lawyer.

Inside the DCO's office, the DCO and the constable were not making any *progress* in their interrogation of Talgon. They wanted him to admit he killed Badaru and made away with his money. That if he admits doing so, he would give them only part of the money and he could keep the rest. They would also allow him to walk out of the station and treat Badaru's killing as another killing by the religious mobs of yesterday. But if he refuses to confess his crime, they would take him out at night and shoot him and claim he was shot while trying to escape from lawful custody or that in fact he was killed by a religious mob.

But Talgon maintained he knew nothing about Badaru's death. 'He was my friend and he was poor; I have no reason to kill him unless you are saying I am mad,' he said

'Why were your eyeglasses found by his dead body if you did not kill him?' asked the constable.

'Like I told you before, we were attacked by religious fanatics at a wedding at Durmi,' said Talgon. 'When I was knocked down, I didn't know where I was or my eyeglasses. When I regained consciousness, all I could do was to get myself and a poor child that was dying under the distress he found himself out of the wedding reception venue to where we could find help. Like I said, Badaru was my friend. It's possible when the eyeglasses fell from me after we were attacked, he saw them and picked them to give me later if I had not been killed in the mayhem.'

Talgon spoke with an innocence and calmness the DCO felt touching. Throughout his career in the police force, he had never handled a suspect with Talgon's unalloyed sincerity, rustic innocence and philosophical calmness and it was making him very uneasy. No one could be telling lies and look the way Talgon was.

But as far as the constable was concerned, Talgon was lying. But he could not employ the means he was adept at to draw the truth out of the suspect without the sanction of the DCO.

For close to an hour, the DCO and the constable asked Talgon all manner of questions all aimed at getting him confess the crime he was suspected of, but he with rare single mindedness stuck to his original story.

'What do you do for a living?' asked the DCO, his eyes probing Talgon's face.

'I used to be in the military,' said Talgon. 'But I left the military long ago. Now I am in business.'

No wonder thought the DCO. No wonder the calmness. No wonder the DPO does not want to be involved in his case. They must have known each other in the army. It would pain him to handle Talgon's case without squeezing something out of him because he knows him. But I who Talgon does not know can squeeze out of him whatever there is to squeeze out without the burden of *esprit de corp*.

When later the DPO came to know that Talgon was

arrested for armed robbery and murder, he patted himself
for having the wisdom to screen himself from his former
colleague. He knew Talgon very well and knew him as an
honest, harmless man. But people do change. Perhaps
Talgon had changed. He would remain behind the screen
and wrap his hands round Talgon's neck until he vomits
the money he had robbed the dead man of.

But the DCO who was to serve as the screen
seemed to be taken by Talgon's innocence and was
unwilling to do the bidding of the DPO. He was a
police officer who believed that it was not in every
case he must extort money from a suspect. Where
a suspect appeared innocent as Talgon, the DCO
would write him off as a bad case and look
towards good cases where he would recoup what
he lost in the bad case.

The DPO, however, was a horse of another
color. Unlike the DCO, he knew of no bad case.
Every case was a good one from which he must
make money. So he kept battering the DCO to step
up pressure on Talgon until he confesses his crime
and handover the money or at least some of it to
them.

But the DCO would not. When the DPO
called him to his office after two days of Talgon's
arrest to know if the suspect was beginning to
cooperate, the DCO told him that Talgon appeared
to him an honest, honorable man that should be
released right away. However, if the DPO wanted
to detain him further, the best thing was to charge

him to court instead of holding him at the police station when the law said he should be taken to court within twenty-four hours of his arrest. Suddenly the atmosphere in the office of the DPO turned icy.

'Charge him to court?' murmured the DPO with an expression that seemed to suggest he held the court in contempt.

'Yes, charge him to court,' said the DCO. 'If we don't do so, his lawyer would charge us.'

'Has he engaged a lawyer?' the DPO asked with a look of alarm.

'It appears he has,' said the DCO. 'The Investigation Officer handling the matter has told me his lawyer is already preparing an application for enforcement of his fundamental human right to liberty in the High Court.'

'And the lawyer has no courtesy of coming to us to hear our own side of the story? Ah ... this job. I sometimes wonder...'

'Most lawyers now consider it beneath their dignity to go to a police station to seek bail. They simply go to the judge who they say is one of them.'

'We are more or less dogs,' lamented the DPO. 'We do the killing; the judges and the lawyers do the cooking and eating. It is so unfair. Ah...'

'But a policeman is meant to be a dog,' said the DCO, his own declaration paining him as if he was forced to make it. But distasteful as what he had just said was to him, this was the way he had always felt about the job. Sometimes in an even more servile manner, what a policeman is required to do is exactly what a dog is required to do for his master.

'How the police job would have been wonderful without the lawyers. How ineffective it is with them,' grumbled the DPO. In a case without a lawyer, it was after they finished milking the cow that they pass it over to the court. But once there was a lawyer, he and the judge his friend would take over the milking. It was so cruel and galling.

'DCO, so what you are saying is that even the milk that we ought to get from a bail application at the station would not be forthcoming,' said the DPO.

'I am afraid that's how the case is shaping up.'

'Fine,' swore the DPO almost panting with anger. 'They have to find him alive before they can bail him.'

Chapter Nineteen

In his cell inside the police station, Talgon's two palms were over his nose and mouth in a vain attempt to cut off the stench in the cell. The stench inside the cell was putrid enough. But the one coming out of the open latrine directly opposite the cell was poisonous. In Talgon's mind, it could not possibly be the smell of human faeces. There must be a decomposing corpse inside that latrine. As if intending to torture the inmates of the cell with the putrid smell, the door of the open latrine directly opposite the cell was left ajar by the constable who last opened it.

The cell was a small filthy room that could hardly accommodate three people. But there were seven inmates in it now. As overcrowded as it was, the inmates were not tormented so much by the lack of space in the cell as by the stench coming into it from the open latrine that was threatening to fumigate them all. An inmate standing behind Talgon unable to stand the stench any more cried out. This brought a constable at the counter to the cell. When he got near the cell, the stench coming out of the open toilet hit him like a pan of shit. He doubled back a few paces, his hands covering his nose and mouth in a futile attempt to cut off the putrid stench. He quickly shut the door of the toilet and turned round to demand of the inmates what the matter was. Like gentle sea waves, anger and suspicion were rolling in his small eyes that when at rest were like tiny chips of ice caved in a mummy.

'That toilet,' said the inmate that cried out. There was now less torture in his voice.

'What's wrong with it?' the constable asked.

His question sounded so stupid to Talgon. 'If nothing is wrong with it, why did you shut it when you came?' he asked.

'Yes, it smells. Since when did criminals win the right to have air-fresheners hung in their stables? You have no more right to complain of the stench coming from this latrine than any rat or cockroach that may happen to lurk around here.' Saying this he opened the toilet again and fled the cell.

But he did not reach the counter before all the inmates by a common impulse of torture cried out in a prolonged roar.

Three policemen at the counter including the constable just returning from the cell rushed to the cell.

On their way to the cell, a police corporal asked the constable that just returned from the cell, 'what's biting them in that cell?'

'I think it's that latrine,' said the constable. It smells bad. And it is open.'

'Why did you not shut it then?' asked the corporal. 'I can see the door open.'

'That will be indulging them. Criminals are

not to be indulged.'

'They are not criminals. They are only suspects.'

'What's the difference?'

'Even criminals are human beings.'

'May be.'

'Tunde, I have always told you that you have a bad mind.'

When they got near the cell, the corporal was so nauseated by the stench coming out of the open latrine that he beat a hasty retreat, his palms over his mouth and nose. He was the most senior police officer on the counter. He immediately sent two junior policemen including Tunde to wash the latrine with *izal* and close the door after washing the toilet. When they were through with their assignment, a new sense of wellbeing enveloped Talgon and his fellow inmates. They were now breathing easily and began to chat among themselves. For a while, they even forgot they were in detention.

'Virtually all of us are in this cell because we can't give the police money to release us,' said one of the inmates. 'It is only in this country that people buy bail as if it were a tuber of yam.'

'And so it is. How I wish I have money to buy bail,' said another inmate.

'But why are our people so corrupt? Everything and everyone is for sale and yet we never seem to get enough money. It's so bad.'

'People are corrupt out of a sense of insecurity,' Talgon said. 'This insecurity is due to the collapse of several commonwealths. For, example, when public schools were well funded and good, there was no need for even rich parents to send their children to private schools. But people in government started stealing the money that was meant to fund public schools and so the public schools were no longer able to give good education. Rich parents started withdrawing their children from the public schools into private schools where good education could be found. This drove people in government to steal more money meant for public schools to send their children to private schools. As it is with education, it is with transportation. The government having killed public transport provided by trains, buses and taxis, forces everyone to own a car. So, everyone must accumulate private wealth to provide his own transportation since there is no commonwealth of public transport. But, private wealth breeds insecurity. It breeds armed robbers, fraudsters, assassins, rapists and arsonists who turn their anger on those they think took their share. The path to security is generating commonwealth which creates private wealth for all. Private wealth does not create commonwealth. We have been doing it the wrong way. Instead of drawing the horse by the head, we are drawing it by the tail. That's why we are booted and bloodied.'

The other inmates began to speak among themselves all at once:

'We have lost our capital – our heads, and so our labor – our bodies, labor in vain.'

'Beside the collapse of commonwealths, what has happened to us to make us so insecure?'

'I think we are driven by greed and ignorance to thoughtlessness so much that we can't see where security is.'

'The solution to our problems is covered by our greed which is under our noses. But because our noses so much like the aroma of greed, instead of sneezing to blow off the cover so that we can see what is under it, we are sniffing like rats to draw the cover and what is under it into our nostrils.'

'You know there is a saying: The bigger the nose the bigger the greed. Greed lives in the nose. It is what is pushing our noses to cover our faces.'

'Let's not be joking over a serious matter; why are we so greedy and selfish?'

'Because there's Bivan's house in us. There is nothing a member of Bivan's house likes like rank. It's his love for rank that drives him to acquire titles. At the root of our problems is our penchant for titles.'

'But why do we so much love rank?'

'I think it's because we are haunted by a collective sense of failure, of lack of achievement in the things that matter.'

'Finding little merit in themselves, the villagers appointed a chief – a sort of barn into which their little worth would collect into a big worth.'

'Now, there is a rat mentality everywhere you turn in this country. Now Bivan's house is a house of rats. A rat mentality can lead to *Black Death*, the sort of death caused by black rats in Europe. As Jews and lepers were attacked in Europe on the outbreak of *Black Death*, so would members of Bivan's house. Never committed to an hour of honest work, everyone is getting so devious in the game of survival.'

'I think the rest of the world needs to quarantine us in this house before we infect it with a flu that has no cure.'

'Lemmings in their search for food move in large flocks towards the coast only to be drowned at sea. We will all be drowned in a sea of corruption.'

'The government creates misery for people.'

'People in government are the big rats cornering everything into their holes.'

'There's a party going on in Bivan's house right now, but the punchbowl is not reaching everyone in the house.'

'But why can't the people rebel?'

'Part of the reason rats cannot rise up against the cat is their dishonesty.'

'Corruption has castrated all of us. We are all

sows without balls between our legs. Our snorting is getting on the nerves of the world.'

'We are suffering so much in this country and whenever there is a little relief, people are happy with the government for being so good. Torture and occasional reprieve from torture have become a strategy of governance in this house.'

'Even in this cell, you can see a bit of what you are saying. The stench of that toilet was released on us and now we have almost forgotten we are in jail unjustifiably because the smell has been withdrawn"

'Public funds arc converted to private wealth and people praise government officials who give them a little of it.'

Chapter Twenty

The DCO of Bangora police station where Talgon was detained was a man who never wanted to hurt honest people. He knew he was not honest and never thought it was possible for any policeman in Bivan's house to be honest. Outside the police, almost everyone he knew and had had dealings with has turned out to be a crook, a shyster and a scoundrel of one sort or the other. It was true when people said honesty in Bivan's house was as scarce as ice water in hell. This meant he must never harm an honest man or allow any harm to come to him, if he could hope for any ice water in this hell. In his mind, if all honest people were to disappear completely leaving only dishonest people, life would become a nightmare if not impossible. So, he had to preserve any honest man that required his preservation. He saw Talgon as an honest man and was determined to ensure no harm befalls him in the police station.

The DPO was a very spiteful and vengeful man when his manoeuvres to extort money from a suspect were thwarted. The DCO could see the DPO's spite and obsession to take his frustration out on Talgon was getting more intense and desperate. Unless he the DCO could devise a way of outwitting him, the DPO might do something rash that would harm Talgon. Somehow, he would have to find a way of stopping the DPO from giving effect to any evil designs he might be developing on Talgon without the DPO knowing it was his scheme that thwarted him. The way the DPO had spoken, the DCO was in no doubt the DPO meant to have Talgon shot dead in the night if in the end he could not extort money from him. Somehow, he would stop that from happening. But how? The DPO was a man who mobilized his energies and genius for vendetta of no material consequence to him as he did for results of great material consequence to him. Right now, he was likely to be in his office scheming with all his intellect and reason in attendance on how to get rid of Talgon in the night without a shadow of suspicion cast on him or a trace of it leading to him.

It did not take the DCO a long time to figure out how to save Talgon. There was no doubt that the DPO knew Talgon which also meant Talgon knew the DPO. He would bring Talgon out of the cell to the counter where the two men would see each other when the DPO was leaving the office for the day. The DCO felt that after Talgon had seen the DPO and spoken to him, much of the passion of the DPO to kill Talgon in cold blood was likely to dissipate.

But at the time he was to bring Talgon out to the counter so that the DPO could not avoid Talgon seeing him when he was going out of the police station after close of work, the DCO was delayed in his office by an old man from his village who wanted him to assist him with money to buy drugs that had been prescribed for him. The old man was a man the DCO always had pity for because of his circumstances. Although the old man was among those that struggled to have a primary school located in the DCO's village, none of his five children went to school beyond the primary school he helped brought to the village. Desperate to have his own child in college, when the son of the old man's relation who was already in a secondary school and who therefore did not need another admission into secondary school wrote the common entrance examination and had a double pass that entitled him to admission into either a central government college or a state secondary school if he passes the two interviews his double pass entitled him, the old man would not agree that his son go for only one interview while the son of another person go for the other. He insisted his son would go for the two interviews. The man whose son was denied attending one of the interviews stoically remarked that though there might be heavy rain clouds in the sky, rain might not necessarily fall. The words of the man turned out to be very prophetic. The son of the old man failed the two interviews and the doors of college remained firmly closed against his children. As primary school leavers, three of the old man's children were waiters in different hotels.

The old man kept lamenting that though he struggled to bring a primary school to his village, it was children of other people that had taken the benefit while his own children were only good for serving beer and clearing cigarette butts from the floors of hotels and restaurants. Whenever the DCO remembered this lamentation of the old man, he was moved to pity for him and as much as it lay in his means, he tried to solve the old man's problems.

When therefore the old man came into his office at the time the DCO wanted to take Talgon to the counter, the DCO could not immediately leave his office. Indeed, for a while, he even forgot about his intention to take Talgon to the counter. So the DPO followed by his orderly who was carrying his bag came down the staircase and walked out of the police station to the porch where his car was waiting for him without the DCO confronting him with Talgon.

In his cell, Talgon was going through a second round of torture after the torture by the stench coming from the open latrine. A couple of hours after the first torture, an inmate who said he was the king of the cell began to torment Talgon who was the latest inmate in the cell. As the friendly and animated conversation the washing and closure of the stinking latrine generated were petering out, a strapping man with bloodshot eyes declared himself the king of the cell whose pleasures other inmates must attend to. He said he had been detained in so many police stations and prisons that he was beginning to lose count. In one prison that he served a three-year term, he was taken to a farm by a prison warder, but was somehow left behind in the farm when the warder was taking the inmates back to the prison. When a headcount of the inmates taken to the farm was taken in the prison and he was missing, it was thought he had run away. But in the morning of the following day, he was knocking at the gate of the prison to be let in. In all prisons or police cells he had stayed, he was king of his cell. In the beginning of his reign in various cells, he usually became king by the strikes of his fists. After fighting and beating other contenders to the throne, he would become king and from that moment all other inmates surrendered their meals to him. It was only after he had eaten to his satisfaction that the other inmates ate the leftover of what he could not eat. Whatever was the leftover, the other inmates were sure there would be no meat in it. With his index finger he would have burrowed through the leftover of the meal to ensure he had not forgotten to pick any tiny piece of meat that may be hidden in some crevice of the food. Meat was only for kings he used to tell his subjects and he was the king. After many sojourns in different prisons and police stations, he no longer had to fight the inmates before he became king of his cell.

His eyes and attitudes had acquired an uncanny effect on other inmates that all he needed to do to become king of a cell was to declare himself king and he would assume the throne. An inmate in a prison cell he was recently said a mere glance into the eyes of the king would show you the devil that lived there.

The king of the cell was brought into the cell moments before Talgon was. Though he was used to the dirt and stench of police and prison cells in Bivan's house, it seemed the stench he met in this police station was more than what he had ever been exposed to. So like other inmates, he gasped and groaned under the stench while it lasted. But when friendly conversations fresh air in the cell had engendered were running out, he declared himself king of the cell. A sinister atmosphere crept into the cell upon this declaration. As he expected, no one protested. Hearing, no protest, the king went on to explain the implications of his kingship to his subjects. All meals were to be surrendered to him. Other inmates were to eat only the leftover of what he could not eat. As they were in a police cell, usually they were to be fed by their relations or by the person upon whose complaint they were arrested and detained. He the king had no relation to bring him food because his relations no longer knew nor cared which prison or police cell he was. So, he expected no food from his relations. Neither had he a complainant that would pay for his feeding. He was arrested by the police when attempting to snatch the handbag of a lady going into a super market. So, if anyone would have to pay for his feeding, it was the police and from his experience, the police bought little food for suspects they arrested. Even when food was brought for a suspect by his relations, the police pinched some of it before passing it over to the suspect. Where a complainant was asked by the police to deposit some money for the feeding of a suspect he had caused the police to arrest, the police pinched some of the money. The long and short of what he was telling his subjects was that he was a man of no expectations other than his expectations of the food that would be brought for other inmates by their relations or bought for them by the police with money complainants had deposited. He said he knew food was not always brought into the cell particularly food brought by relations of a suspect. Often the suspect was taken to the counter to eat his food and for his relations to see and talk to him. If any suspect was taken to the counter to eat food brought by his relations and he ate it there, he would cut open the stomach of the suspect when he returned to the cell and eat his own share. He produced a knife so embedded in his loin as to be part of his body. Although no suspect believed he would do what he threatened, they all knew he would make such a suspect suffer so much that he would have been better off without the food. When a suspect was given any food at the counter, he must bring the food to the cell and give it to him. At night, the other inmates were to lie on each other to sleep to create room for the king to sleep well. Without warning, he slapped Talgon and asked him to kneel down.

Talgon was as stunned by the fact that the slap was

unprovoked as by its severity.

'You look to me the greenhorn here. So, you need some lessons of life in the home of the forsaken,' he said, baring his bloodshot eyes at Talgon and squeezing his lips into a vicious snarl of a monster giving lessons he has received from the devil.

In the silence that followed, Talgon and the other inmates seemed to feel more keenly the breathing menace in their midst.

'You look too innocent for this place,' he said to Talgon, poking his ribs with his forefinger. 'Swear you will not infect us with your innocence or contaminate this place with your gentleman manners!'

Talgon did not say anything.

'It's getting too cold. Remove your shirt and give it to me!' the king of the cell commanded Talgon in a voice that carried a whip. The shirt he was wearing not only carried the shadows of all the prisons its owner had been wearing it, but seemed to have been worn by those prisons as much as by the man now wearing it. The king of the cell looked every inch like the devil's orderly and affected his air.

Talgon lucky to be wearing a vest removed his shirt and gave it to the king of the cell who put it on, smirking at him.

The king of the cell impressed Talgon as a man whose criminality was now for the prison and police cells and not for the outside world.

Chapter Twenty-One

Outside the police station an event unrelated to Talgon's arrest and detention but would lead to his release had just taken place. It was close to *Eid-el Kabir* sallah festival. Three people went to a small village and told the villagers they had been sent by the common calabash of Bangora Local Government to buy thirty rams which he intended to share to people for the festival. They said the thirty rams would only be paid for when taken to the common calabash in his house. Thirty fat rams were loaded into a lorry and two unsuspecting villagers were asked to follow the three strangers to collect the money of the rams from the common calabash. However, deep into a forest on their way, the strangers stopped the lorry and ordered the villagers at gunpoint to disembark from the lorry. The villagers thoroughly scared, disembarked frantically. Firing into the air, the lorry took off with the rams bleating and the villagers running helter-skelter into the bush.

When news of what happened got to the common calabash of Bangora Local government, he was enraged. His immediate impulse was to call the DPO to his office to know what his men were doing to track down the miscreants, but on a second thought, he felt he could make some political capital out of this misfortune by trekking to the police station to see the DPO. Already his name had been smeared and scandalized by the cheats. Though everyone knew the miscreants were not sent by him, but the scandalous atmosphere they had created around him still hung over his head like a dark cloud. He would help dispel this atmosphere by some theatrical actions he takes. Trekking to the DPO's office recommended itself to him as an appropriate theatrical action to take. So, with some members of his Council, he walked to the police station which was not too far from the Council secretariat to see the DPO.

As the common calabash had expected, as he and his Council members walked to the police station from the secretariat, they were followed by a crowd of people most of whom joined them on the road so that by the time they reached the police station, they had packed a thundering crowd behind them. Most of the people following the common calabash had already heard what happened and suspected he was going to the police station to see the DPO over what they had heard. But what most people did not understand was why the common calabash was going to see the DPO when he had the option of calling the latter to his office. What they understood even less was why the common calabash should trek to the police station when he should be in a jeep or some other exotic car.

'Two weeks ago, five people wearing the traditional dress of courtiers in the palace of the Emir of Gomka gained access into the house of the ceremonial feast for internal affairs who is from Gomka,' said one of the people following the common calabash to the police station to his friend. 'The security men at the gate believing the men were sent by the emir to see the ceremonial feast as they claimed opened the gate for them and even gave them a royal salute. But no sooner were the men inside the premises that things began to happen. The five men carrying arms under their flowing robes brought out their guns and easily overpowered the security men who were not in the least expectation of danger. The armed robbers made away with forty million baduns from the ceremonial feast's house.'

'I heard that story, but my wonder then and even now is how the ceremonial feast had so much money in his house,' said the friend.

'How can you wonder how a ceremonial feast would have as much as forty million baduns in his house when even a local government common calabash can have so much?' The words *local government common calabash* were pronounced in a whisper.

'The arrow from your brother's bow knows where your heart is and will always find it. You are seldom succeeded against without the help of your brother. Hunters are always led into the jungle by dogs which know the hiding places of the games.'

'I think in this country, we are in guerrilla warfare for economic resources and not for political power.'

'I rather think we are in a rat-race. I believe you have heard the story of what a pastor who after offerings were made in his church and the congregation dispersed leaving him alone with the money did with the money.'

'I have not heard the story. Please, can you tell me?'

'When the pastor was left alone with the money, he said, "God, this money is for you in heaven and I your servant on earth. Now I will throw the whole money into the sky so that you take what belongs to you. Whatever falls to the ground is mine your servant on earth."

Many people walking close to the two friends who heard the story laughed. Several commentaries sprung up from the story that had just been told.

'The cunning of that pastor smokes a long pipe.'

'It is the harvest of an old tortoise.'

'I think it is a breathing menace.'

'Even the white man cannot deny we are more innovative than him in certain things.'

'Only rats fight for survival the way we do.'

'Armed robbers perhaps hearing the story of

the cunning pastor stormed a church some weeks ago in Jalam shortly after offering. They said since the money was for God, they would take it to him in heaven and spare the pastor the labor.'

'The vulture by his opportunism is feasting on the ruins of his preys without pity; the tortoise by his cunning is running faster than the antelope to collect, without remorse, prizes he has not won and the rat by his thievery is filling his barns with the harvest of the rabbit without regret.'

'When kerosene is cheap, petrol vendors mix it with petrol killing the engines of cars of those unfortunate to buy their petrol.'

'When petrol is cheaper than kerosene, sellers of kerosene mix it with petrol setting ablaze the houses of those who buy kerosene from them.'

'Palm oil sellers mix their oil with poisonous substances to increase its quantity. Those who consume such oil, suffer from one grave ailment or the other.'

'Close to Salah festivals, ram sellers who are mostly Moslems feed their rams with chaff and potash which generate a lot of thirst in the rams. The rams are then given drums of water to drink to bloat out their tummies and give them the appearance of fat rams. This way, buyers are deceived into buying big barrels of water thinking they are buying meat. For all they may not know, the conmen who went to that village and used the name of the common calabash to deceive the villagers into parting with their rams might have made away with drums of water, not the meat they thought.'

A month ago, a friend told me he was on the way to Hemdo in the south when the luxurious bus he was travelling in was stopped by armed robbers. All passengers on board were commanded to disembarked. The armed robbers asked those with money to queue on one line and those without money on another. When passengers on the queue of those without money were searched for money by one of the armed robbers, a man with money was found on the queue. While flogging him, the leader of the armed robbers was chiding him as a man without the least honesty. He went on to lament that it was dishonest people like the passenger he was flogging that have prevented the nation from making progress.'

'What of the student who failed his exams, and upon his father demanding to know why, he said he bought the wrong answers.'

'Yesterday truth and lies visited Bivan's house from a faraway country. The two visitors knocked on the door of the house, but the door was only opened for lies. Poor truth had to walk away, famished and scorned by a hostile host. Poor truth slept out of doors hungry and miserable. But today it is happy. It woke up this morning to hear the host that turned it away yesterday quarrelling with his guest – lies.'

'What is really happening in Bivan's house?' someone asked, rhetorically.

'Bivan's house is ablaze with corruption. The roaring flames are licking the sky like the seared bottom of a pot.'

'God may have to snatch his legs from the leaping flames or he would be singed.'

'Bivan's house is a rotten cow vultures and hyenas are feeding on without anyone shouting haa!'

'Fakers, scammers, conmen, moral derelicts of all kind are on the loose in the country like loose cannons.'

'If it were only in the country, it wouldn't have been so bad. You suffer little shame if your child steals only in your house. But when he goes outside to steal, your shame can be quite pressing.'

'Corruption is the sticking point holding us where we are. It is the monkey on our back that is holding us to the mud. The big signature that defines all of us is F-R-A-U-D. This is the impress by which we are recognized by the rest of the world. This is the basket we are all collected in.'

'Among the politicians of Bivan's house, it is only Jamimi you can point to as a man whose conscience has not fled him.'

'We are in for it.'

'Is it only us that are in for it? The whole world is in for it with us. We are killing the goose that laid the golden eggs.'

'Cut off from what is right, we know not what is wrong and so shrines are built for the devil where churches and mosques used to be!'

'We all admire fraud in this country. Those who stay out of it do so out of cowardice not out of moral choice. Since it has always been the place of cowardice to admire courage, those who have the courage to be crooks are admired by those who fear to be crooks.'

'I believe the owl has made his nest in Bivan's house. In my village, the owl is the harbinger of evil.'

'We are lost. Who will find us?'

'It depends where you are lost and how far you are lost. If you are lost far in the jungle, you are lost for good. No one can ever find you.'

'After the death of a village head, the chief priest of Konga village declares who the gods have chosen to be the new village head. It was a taboo for any heir to the throne to bribe the chief priest to declare him the choice of the gods. But on the death of his father who was village head, Wakum the youngest of the children of the late village head went and bribed the chief priest who declared him the new village head. As soon as he became village head, Wakum started talking of the sanctity of the taboo that forbade bribing the chief priest to the hearing of his subjects who suspected he ascended the throne through foul means.'

'What is particularly frightening is that

nemesis doesn't seem to catch up with evil doers any more. Before it was not like that. An evil doer was certain to be visited by nemesis sooner or later, but often sooner than later. Not so these days. Now people commit the most heinous crimes and live out their full lives without any misfortune lighting upon them. The fear of nemesis which used to restrain people from evil is now gone and society is now left only at the mercy of conscience and fear of the hereafter.'

'I am not in any way surprised by the departure of nemesis. Nemesis as I understand it was brought about by the resentment of a moral community against evil and not by God as we thought. Today there may still be resentment of evil by the community; but the resentment is not by a moral community, but by an immoral one. Resentment by this type of community can no more produce nemesis than a blown-out fuse produce light.'

'The mores of our forebears were the shrines from which nemesis used to visit the wicked. The rain and wind of anomie have destroyed these shrines leaving relics you can only find in abandoned ancestral homelands. Because gods do not live outside like hyenas, reward and nemesis the oracles in the shrines of the mores of our forebears had fled leaving us victims without avengers.'

Chapter Twenty-Two

The common calabash seeing the huge crowd he had collected on his way to the police station was immensely pleased he took the decision he took. The multitude behind him meant he was still popular with the people. Elections were not far off and he wanted to contest for the office of common calabash again. What he was seeing now was a good omen for this ambition. But as it is commonly said, *if a man is handsome, he should enhance his handsomeness with bathing regularly*. When he gets to the police station, he would do something radical that would make him more popular with the people. Like every police station in Bivan's house, the police station at Bangora was a prison of some sort where suspects were detained indefinitely under torturous conditions without being charged to court. The official excuse for not charging suspects to court often given by the police was that they were still investigating their cases, still gathering evidences with which to prosecute the suspects. But in private, some policemen argued that it did not matter much charging suspects to court since the courts hardly sit. Others lamented that charging a suspect to court meant submitting themselves to be messed up by lawyers and judges. Most of the detained suspects were detained over flimsy allegations;

others out of sheer mischief. When he gets to the police station, he would demand to know how many suspects were in the police station and why they were being detained. If the police could not justify the detention of a suspect, he would order his release. As a student in the university, he was one of the students that went to the Kanga grain board, broke into it and distributed the grains to the poor because people were dying of hunger. He was also among the students that stormed a prison and released all the prisoners because as he and his fellow students reasoned, it was unjust to keep petty criminals in prison while big criminals that stole public funds were moving freely about town. Today he would enact a feat akin to that. For a while he was moved to contempt for the current crop of students for their imbecility that made them capable of rioting only over religious sentiments. But when he remembered how their imbecility was playing to his advantage as a common calabash that was not doing much for his people, he smiled to himself.

The common calabash met the DPO in front of the police station. The noise of the people following the common calabash had brought the DPO from his office overlooking the approach to the police station to the front of the station. At first, he was alarmed when he saw such a mammoth crowd moving towards the station. But when he saw the Local Government common calabash walking in front of the crowd, he was relieved. But why should the common calabash be coming to the police station instead of calling him as he had always done? How could a whole local government common calabash with all the money of the Local Government under his control condescend to come to the police station to see a mere DPO like him? More puzzling and troubling was that the common calabash was not only coming to the station on foot but leading a huge crowd. What was all this intriguing spectacle about? Could it be over the rams' scandal? But why should what is a regular occurrence in Bivan's house spark up a drama such as the one he was beholding? Even the Central Bank Governor of Bivan's house had been scandalized by conmen that held themselves out in Germany as his representatives and swindled a multinational corporation of seventy million dollars. That did not spark up a riot like what he was seeing coming towards the station. Well, whatever it was, the common calabash on who he depended for handouts must not be suffered to come up to his office upstairs or to call him downstairs. He would receive him in front of the station. So he came to the front of the station.

It was like the DPO had pre-empted the common calabash's action. The common calabash had no intention of climbing up to the DPO's office. He would call the DPO to the front of the station and do everything before the people. This way he would achieve the effect he wanted to by coming to the station the way he did.

In front of the police station, before the crowd with him, the common calabash demanded to know if the fraudsters that scandalized his name had been arrested.

'We are still doing our best to apprehend them sir,' the DPO said. 'Sooner or later, I believe my men would round them up.'

'Since the police clearly are failing to discharge their responsibilities of maintaining law and order, I am beginning to wonder if we shouldn't start paying the armed robbers and fraudsters or even the dogs to protect us,' said the common calabash with a faint smile on his lips.

The crowd ululated and cheered.

'Well, let's leave this thought for another day,' continued the common calabash. 'Now how many suspects do you have in this station?'

The DPO was shocked by this unexpected question and for a while he could not say anything.

'Mr. DPO, *ogar* is waiting for an answer from you,' said a Council member the common calabash sometimes gave money to give the DPO. There was no mistaking the contempt in his voice and countenance.

'I cannot say exactly, sir. But I am sure the DCO and the administrative officer will know,' said the DPO, lacking most of the comportment and authority of his office. He turned to the DCO who was standing beside him to know how many detainees they had at the station.

'Thirty-nine,' said the DCO.

'Thirty-nine!' the common calabash exclaimed, his eyes popping out. 'I am not sure there are more prisoners in the prison of this town.'

The crowd hissed and jeered.

The common calabash was elated. He was obviously putting up a good performance. 'How many of these suspects detained in your station do you have the least evidence of their being culpable of the offences alleged against them?'

Though there were many suspects the DCO knew were detained in the station on mere rumor of committing one offence or the other, it was only Talgon who he had adjudged an honest man that he had sympathy for. So, when the common calabash asked him this question it was only Talgon that came to his mind. 'One,' he said.

'Bring that one here,' said the common calabash.

Talgon was immediately brought from his cell by the DCO. Even before he was brought, the DPO suspected he was the one the DCO was referring to given the earlier case he had made for his release. With the common calabash standing with him, he knew he could no longer avoid Talgon seeing him. He braced himself for the encounter.

It happened that some people in the crowd that came to the police station with the common calabash knew Talgon. Their first reaction on seeing him was shock that he was a detainee in a police station. When they overcame their shock, they were not surprised that the DCO brought him out as the detainee against whom the police had the least evidence of crime.

The DPO on his part having seen Talgon being brought out of the police station by the DCO cast his gaze away, giving the impression his attention was on a faraway object and so he had not seen Talgon. But Talgon on coming closer saw him and immediately recognized him.'Emeka!' he called the DPO by his name, quite surprised to see the DPO. 'What are you doing here?'

'Talgon!' exclaimed the DPO, putting on a look of surprise.

'So, you two know each other?' the common calabash asked amused by the unfolding drama.

'We were both in the army before we eventually left to pursue other careers,' said the DPO with what sounded like a nostalgic note in his voice. 'Talgon, I am the new DPO here,' he said, addressing Talgon. 'Why were you arrested and brought here?' he asked with the air and attitude of one somewhat embarrassed to find a friend in an untoward condition.

'It's a long story,' said Talgon. 'But I know I am innocent and innocence will vindicate me.'

'Innocence has already vindicated you,' said the common calabash. 'You can go home. There is no reason honest people should be in detention while criminals are roaming free; or what do you say DPO?'

'Sure, sure,' said the DPO. 'I knew him in the army as an honest man and since the DCO who knows more about the facts and circumstances of his arrest and detention said he is innocent, sure, he can go home. If we need him in future, I believe the DCO has his contact address through which we can find him; is it not so DCO?'

The DCO first nodded his head before saying that Talgon's address and telephone number were on the written statement he made to the police.

Chapter Twenty-Three

Although the order for Talgon's release was made in the evening, he was not released until in the night. The investigation police officer handling his case who was asked to perform some paper formalities and release to him any properties of his with the police did not discharge his assignment until in the night. Despite the fact that he had been ordered to release Talgon, he still wanted to extort some money from him. It was only when it became clear to him that Talgon had no money that he released him. Having no money to board a bus, he began walking home. On the way he saw a rowdy crowd under a lighted street lamp. By the chaotic nature of the crowd and loud noise coming from it, it looked like some people were fighting and the crowd had sprung up around them. Usually, he kept his distance from such crowds because more often than not, they were scams created by crooks to lure innocent people into seeking to offer help only to be dispossessed of their money or some other valuable possessions they might be carrying. A ginger trader who had just sold his ginger and was hurrying home with the money and the empty sacks he carried the ginger to the market saw two men fighting. Not knowing they were thieves who wanted to dispossess him of his money, he went to separate them. Before he knew what was happening, they had pinched his money and one of the empty sacks he was carrying was pulled down his head to his waist. By the time he struggled out of the sack, the two thieves had disappeared with his money. Thinking of this incidence, reminded him of a similar incidence, though not involving people fighting, in which a man who had just collected his salary was lured into losing it by a gesture of kindness by a man who in fact was a thief. Two buttons near the neck of the man had unhooked and the thief pretending to be a caring person approached him saying, 'let me fix your buttons for you.' The man, not knowing he was being conned, cocked his head to one side and presented his neck like a sheep about to be slaughtered to the thief. Moments after leaving the thief, his hand went to his front pocket to feel the money, but the money was gone.

'Well, I have no money,' Talgon muttered to himself as he moved towards the crowd. 'Right now, I am a man who has nothing to lose and may sleep beside the thief without a care.' For days, he had been locked out of life in Bivan's house. The urge to be involved with people outside the police cell was so compelling. When he got closer to the crowd, his suspicion was confirmed. Two men were fighting and as was usual with such scenes, a big crowd had swelled up around the two men. However, by the time Talgon reached the crowd the two men had been separated, but were still hurling insults at each other. The punches, scratches and bites that could not be delivered with the hand, fingers and teeth were now being delivered with the tongue.

'Vulture seller!'

'Fake currency dealer!'

'By your face I should have known you are a vulture. While still living, your head deserves to be eaten by termites.'

'Thief!'

'Rogue!'

By a man at the edge of the crowd, Talgon was told the cause of the fight. A man thought to be selling roasted chickens had sold a roasted vulture to a man who thought he was buying a roasted chicken. The man who bought the roasted *chicken* bought it with a fake five hundred baduns note. The man who sold the vulture went home happy he had cheated the man who bought the *chicken* only to find the *chicken* was bought with a fake currency. The man who bought the vulture with the fake five hundred baduns note went home happy he had cheated the man who sold the *chicken* to him only to find he bought a vulture. Annoyed that they had been cheated, the two men went out looking for each other and when they found each other, a fight erupted.

'You are a crook and a cheat.'

'You are a worse crook.'

'You are a criminal.'

'You are a bastard and a degraded beast.'

Talgon was faintly happy the words *crook* and *criminal* still carried their original meaning in Bivan's house hence they were still being used the way they were now. For sometime, he had been under the haunting fear that Bivan's house full of scammers and fakers, the words *crook* and *criminal* were daily losing the resentment and revulsion they used to spark in the minds of people. He feared that the loss of values in Bivan's house was fast leading to the loss of meaning by certain words. Meaning is only but an expression of values. Meaning grows on values as much as grasses grow on the soil. Therefore, an attack on values is an attack on meaning. Having desecrated values, he could see members of Bivan's house desecrating meaning. So hearing the two fighting men who had just been separated calling each other *criminal* and *crook* in the hope of hurting each other was heart-warming to him. It meant Bivan's house was not totally lost yet.

Talgon got to his house to find his mother who had been told of his incarceration in a police station and his wife who had told her out of their wits ends on how to get him out of detention. His mother was not a woman of many words, but in time of trouble, she was a dependable pillar. She was an empathetic woman very resentful of corruption. Those who knew her said Talgon inherited his empathy and distaste for corruption from her. Although she was now an old woman, she had lost little of her passion to help others and little of her hate of what her moral code did not approve. But Talgon's wife did not tell his father or her own mother what had happened because she knew they would not get any sympathy from these two.

It might be said of Talgon's father that although he set out to be an honest and empathetic man, along the way he was discouraged by the dishonesty and ill-use he suffered in the hands of others. Because of what he had gone through in life, he became cynical towards honesty, if not contemptuous of it. After his secondary school, he was employed by the Scholarship Board of his state. They were supposed to report for training on a particular date, but could not due to certain logistics the Scholarship Board said it could not overcome. When eventually they reported, they were paid four thousand baduns for the three weeks they were not on training. He returned his own money saying he had not earned it. He was laughed and scoffed at by other recruits who said he was a mad man. To weed out ghost workers, the state government occasionally made table payments to workers in ministries, parastatals and boards suspected to be harboring ghost workers. Everyone had to present himself and his identity card for payment. Whoever did not appear was treated as a ghost worker and his name was knocked off the payroll of his office. In one of such payments in the Scholarship Board, he not counting his money well thought he had been overpaid. He returned two hundred baduns to the paying officer. But when he returned to his office and counted the money again, he discovered he made a mistake in his first counting. He was not overpaid. He went back to the paying officer hoping to be given back the two hundred baduns, but the paying officer said he could not even remember he had returned any money to him. In another table payment, he was underpaid by the payment officer and all his complaints that he had been underpaid fell on deaf ears. Komau's breach of trust and betrayal of confidence finally made him spurn honesty and trust. Komau – his friend staying with him ran away with scholarship money he kept in his house. They had gone to pay university students their scholarship allowance, but could not exhaust the money they took with them because it was discovered that some of the students in the payroll did not exist. His colleagues said they should share the money among themselves, but he refused. So, the money was brought back to be returned to the Board. Since they got back to their station after close of work, the money was left with him to bring to the office the following day. The following day, the money was gone and Komau his friend with it. When he reported what had happened in the office the following day, no one believed him. His colleagues, who had proposed they share the money, accused him in secret that he had refused them sharing the money so that he would corner the whole thing for himself. He was given two weeks to return the money, failing which he was dismissed. He became brokenhearted and since then had been indifferent to honesty and helping others. In his old age, he seemed to have moved from indifference to honesty and empathy to hostility. Talgon first had a glimpse of his attitude to empathy when at school he wrote to him saying: 'Daddy, condition at school critical; suicide contemplated.' He wrote back saying: 'Son, condition at home more critical; suicide approved.'

To his displeasure, his son Talgon seemed to be treading the path of honesty and empathy that had led to his ruin. He blamed his wife for this. She was the one that had misled him into a path no one was following in Bivan's house.

'Stay away from honesty,' he always admonished his son 'It will do you no good. It has never done any man any good, at least in Bivan's house. Think not of fighting corruption because you have no fighting chance against it. Help no one because no one will help you. Cheat if you can because you will be cheated if you cannot. This is the only way you will not return home by the weeping cross.'

Talgon's wife knew that if she went to his father and told him what had happened the old man would assume it was Talgon's honesty or sympathy for others that had gotten him into trouble as usual. He would laugh and say, 'I told him. Now look at it. If he would not learn by commonsense, he would learn by tears; if he would not learn by tears, he would learn by blood.' So she had avoided him and told his mother only. But the father was to later hear what happened and went to see the son.

Chapter Twenty-Four

The little child begging for alms looked hungry, threadbare and abandoned. Looking like he ate nothing last night, the little child looked like he did not sleep either. As Talgon's father was about boarding the bus that would take him to his son's house, the little child looking forsaken by the world moved towards him with a begging bowl in his eyes and hands. The old man's heart quaked with sympathy as he watched the little child walking sheepishly and haltingly towards him. But he quickly rebuked his heart and walked away from the bus he was about boarding. Further down the road, he flagged down another bus that was swaying and creaking on the road under the weight of age, lack of maintenance and overloading. The only space left in the bus was a little opening between the bus conductor sitting on the bus engine and two passengers sitting on the engine with him. He entered and sat where the bus conductor indicated to him and the bus began its torturous and mournful journey again.

Talgon was at home when the old man arrived. His father was a man with a lot of charm and atmosphere. When he walked into his house, his charm and atmosphere like a siren announced his presence. After Talgon narrated his ordeal to him, the old man shook his head and for a long time sat with his head bowed and his shoulders hunched like the props of a scarecrow. He suddenly looked very old to Talgon.

'I have told you never to help anyone and to stay away from honesty, but you will not listen to me,' the old man began to speak very slowly. Although an old man, his voice was surprisingly young. To his amusement, a friend once told him his voice was like an oasis of youth surrounded by a desert of old age.

'Honesty and helping others ruined my life,' continued the old man in his unusually young voice. 'See where I am now. I could not train you and your younger sister up to the university because of honesty and trying to help others. Don't allow what happened to me happen to you. You have a son in the university; follow the path everyone is following in this country and train him. From following honesty, I returned home by the weeping cross when there was nobody at home to carry the cross off my shoulders. Don't allow that to happen to you.'

'Not everyone in Bivan's house is following the path you are recommending to me,' Talgon said, avoiding the old man's piercing eyes.

'Who else is on that path with you?'

'Jamimi is on the same path with me.'

'Jamimi is a politician and I believe he is playing politics with honesty,' said the old man, gnashing his teeth. 'Very soon the wind will blow and the anus of the fowl would be exposed.'

'There is no water along the path you are recommending for me,' Talgon said, his face averted from the probing eyes of the old man.

'And you think there is water along your own path?' asked the old man, his eyes pecking Talgon's face. 'Look here my son, this is the devil's country and the devil is taking care of his own. Don't be a fool.'

'Those who are dishonest gain from dishonesty because there are people who are honest.'

'Well said,' said the old man. 'Let us then all be dishonest so that dishonesty will no longer work for anyone.'

'Everywhere lemmings are known for mass migration in search of food. In search of food, lemmings follow each other to their common ruin. No lemming goes out of line out of fear of missing out on any food the flock may find only for all the lemmings to perish in a common disaster. I can see you are trying to turn me into a lemming. But I can't be what you want me to be. I will not bend my knee to corruption nor pay homage to dishonesty,' said Talgon, defiantly.

'You know of lemmings and yet said there is no water along the path I am asking you to follow? Lemmings if you don't know always move towards the sea.'

'Where they will be drowned, you should add.'

'That's the vain thought of people like you. No lemming has ever been drowned by moving towards the sea. At any rate, it is better to die in a group at sea than alone in the desert.'

'Perhaps some people feel better dying with others; but for me mass death is more horrifying than dying alone. I will never be a lemming.'

'You see, when the tortoise wants to embark on a senseless journey, whatever you tell him, he will not hear until he has received his disgrace,' said the father, a resigned expression on his face. 'I can see you are even worse than the tortoise. You are already receiving your disgrace, but it seems you are not ready to listen to sense and return from your senseless journey.'

'Father, the problem is that you were extreme in your pursuit of honesty when you believed in honesty. Now spurning honesty, you are extreme in doing so. In everything, moderation is what keeps us from regret.'

'Perhaps I was extreme in my pursuit of honesty. But are you not also extreme in your trudge on that untrodden path? When I was extreme as you said, there was more honesty in Bivan's house than there is today. Today honesty in this house is as scarce as ice water in hell. This country is hell. If you are ice water, the devil and his demons will exhaust you in one quaff.'

'But it's someone's help − at least the common calabash's help that brought me out of the police cell today,' Talgon said. 'Everyone is not rotten.'

'That's where you are wrong again. You are not out of detention because of the common calabash's benevolence, but because of the scandal of the fraudsters that brought the common calabash to the police station in the first place. Those conmen actually released you. You see how things work in this house? Those who are honest have to rely on criminals for their salvation. Public office looters, thieves, fraudsters − the lepers of yesterday, are the kings of today. My son,' continued the old man in a voice cracking with feelings. 'Listen to the words of an old man and you will perch on a fruitful tree. Refuse to listen to them and you will perch on an *akase* tree. Listen to this poem I recently composed on my regrets for not being a leper:

If only I were a leper ...
I won't be eating from the same bowls with dogs
Or fasting when a pillar is not upon me
I won't be going through refuse dumps
With a siren of flies in my ears
As if I were some garbage royalty.

If only I were a leper ...
I will be the chief of my village
Yet, in my village there was a time
No one talked to the leper
No one shook hands with the leper
The leper had no fingers anyway.

If I were a leper in those healthy days of my village
Like all lepers I would have been kept out of the village
But in these sick days of my village
Lepers keep the rest of us out of the village
Today the leper is king
And we are all whimpering under his whip.

Were I a leper ...
In a flash I will erase my shack
And raise a castle on the ruins
In my castle I will speak to God
And men will face my castle in reverence
Every time they pray to God.

If only I were a leper ...
The color of my car
Must match the color of my dress
In these wily days of the chameleon
Color misleads arrows
And wastes the soldier ant in a pond.

If only I were a leper
Ah ... I forgot
In those sunny days in my village
Takai the last leper we drove out of my
village to the jungle
We threw him out with long sticks
In mortal disgust and revulsion.

If only I were a leper ...
Oh no, Takai the last leper we chased out of
my village into the wilds
Lived with the hyena and the vulture in the
jungle
And grew claws where he had no fingers
With his claws in white gloves
The leper came back for the village.

If only I were a leper ...
Yes, I can still remember the admiration for the leper
That returned to my lost village in white gloves
Everyone in my dark village is dazzled
By the gloves of the man
Everyone knows is a leper.

If only I were a leper
Those who could not shake hands with the leper yesterday
Are falling over themselves today
To give their daughters in marriage
To the gentleman in white gloves
Glory now resides with the dung beetle.

If only I were a leper
But there are rumor s the leper is a vampire
Who cares
The gloves on the leper's hands is the Golden Calf
To the little Jews of my wayward village
Where mammon seduces the priest's wife.

If only I were a leper ...
Those I gorged on their blood the previous night
Will cry to me in the morning to save them

The grass will thank the cow
For the fart and muck
Hissing and dripping from the cow's behind.

If only I were a leper ...
I will be an angel from hell
That steals with the squirrel and mourns with
the rabbit
That runs with the hare and hunts with the
hounds
That hoots with the owl and chirrups with the
doves
That loots with brigands and hoods with the
monks.

If only I were a leper ...
My child wouldn't have died of malaria before
my eyes
Because I have no money to buy quinine to
treat him
If only I were a leper ...
I will snap fingers I don't have
And people with fingers will fall at my feet
without toes.

Where is the leper?
Where is the leper? the fellow asked again
Yes, where is the leper?
See him behind you holding the village purse
If only I were a leper ...

Heaven, if only I were a leper ...

In spite of himself, Talgon was moved to tears by this poem that expressed his father's cynicism and regrets for his honest past. 'I still believe I was freed by the common calabash,' he said when he was able to compose his feelings to talk.

'Perhaps, the common calabash helped you,' said the old man. 'But what is the worth of his help compared to what you suffered because you tried to help others? Like I always tell you, stay away from honesty and help no one because no one will help you. If you will not learn by commonsense, you will learn by tears; if you will not learn by tears, you will learn by blood. Since Achimo the former primehead of this country tried to bring honesty and discipline back and failed, I have composed a song for this country. My song which I titled *a worm in the sun* is as true of this country as dirt is of the refuse dump:

There is a rag
Sodden with dirt
Lying in the sun
That rag is a worm
Writhing in the sun
Refusing to live
And refusing to die
Phoebus patriotic spirit
Fell on the worm

And shook it
Laying off
The death-inducing dirt
And let the worm live
But alas
You worm...
You worm writhing in the sun...

'This song should be the national anthem of Bivan's house,' said Umaru who was present when Talgon's father was talking. More than our national anthem, it sums up the condition of Bivan's house.'

After singing his song, Talgon's father walked out of the house without further word to anyone. Moments after, Talgon's cell phone rang.

Well, who can it be? he wondcrcd picking the phone. It was Beckin.

'Why have you not bothered to call me since you left my house?' she whined.

'Because I have been in a police cell since I left your house,' Talgon said.

'What!'

'I was arrested by the police shortly after I left your house.'

'What for?'

'They accused me of murdering my friend Badaru, something I know nothing of.'

'There is no one to mourn for another then,' moaned Beckin. 'The man I used to give money to buy grains for me has absconded with my money.'

'That's terrible. Why should he do such a thing?'

'This is Bivan's house. And this is a man I have being dealing with for the past three years.'

'I am really sorry,' said Talgon, feeling very wretched. 'What of the boy I left with you?' he asked, though he knew in her current state of mind, the child was not likely to be her concern.'

'That child?' Beckin snorted.

'Yes, that child.'

'He left yesterday because I have no food to give him.'

'And you allowed him to go?' Talgon asked, his heart pounding hard.

'But I told you I had no food to give him. Would you rather I kept him so that he starved to death?'

'No.'

'Fine. Besides, I kept him with me because of you. For days, you have been away without a word from you. Thinking you had abandoned us, I began to resent his presence. So, when he said he would go, I allowed him; in fact, I urged him to. Sorry, I am out of airtime.'

'Hello,' Talgon said, but the line was dead. 'This is a cruel world,' he murmured, swirling a vacant look about him, a visibly disturbed expression branded across his face like Kiyak tribal marks. 'Poor child. Poor little boy.' For a long time, he thought about the child wandering the streets of Bangora alone, hungry, homeless and uncared for. He was so depressed as to feel sick. He stood up and walked to the front of his house and sat down on the veranda of the house. After thinking of the child for a while, his mind was seized by what his father told him before he left his house moments ago. How can Bivan's house ever come out of the hole it was? he wondered, his back against the wall of his house. Why should Bivan's house be different from other nations? Where will dishonesty leave this house? When and where will it all end?

From behind the house facing his house, a rat ran along the small path dividing the two houses before disappearing into a hole further off.

'This is it!' Talgon swore. 'This is it! We are done for.'